peach tree city
PEACHTREE CITY LIBRARY
201 Willowbend Road
Peachtree City, GA 30269

NEW TALES FOR OLD

By
George Sharp

Illustrated by
Marjorie M. Sharp

DORRANCE & COMPANY, INCORPORATED
828 LANCASTER AVENUE • BRYN MAWR, PENNSYLVANIA 19010
Publishers Since 1920

Author's Note

This is a work of fiction, and any resemblance between the characters in this book and real persons, whether living or dead, is purely coincidental.

ISBN 0-8059-2965-7
Printed in the United States of America
First Printing

To Marjorie

Acknowledgments

I wish to thank the Reverend John E. Lamb, Librarian of the Episcopal Divinity School in Cambridge, Massachusetts, for providing the rich and valuable source material I needed to present the story of *Waet and the Boy Bishop* in as historically accurate a setting as possible. I am also indebted to the staff of the Media-Upper Providence Free Library for their patience in helping me find points of information for use in writing several of the stories.

George Sharp

Contents

Waet and the Boy Bishop	1
Beyond the Castle Wall	23
The Tree of Bells	55
Two Buttons	91
The Princess with Wooden Ears	123

Waet and the Boy Bishop

England—924 A.D.

Snow sifted through the cracks of the wooden shutters covering the window in Waet's dark, cold cell. The flame of his dish lamp was bright enough for him to see his work as he copied, letter by letter, the writing on the page before him. Every now and then he cupped his hands over the flame of the lamp—but it did little to warm his fingers and he returned to his task, stiff-jointed and aching.

Like other boys in the choir school, he was learning the fine art of copying pages from the Gospels, a useful occupation to be followed after his voice changed and he was no longer able to sing in the cathedral choir.

Unlike the other choristers, Waet was neither Saxon nor Dane in appearance. His red hair and green eyes inherited from his Celtic mother marked him as different from his friends, though his father was a Saxon warrior in the service of Athelstan, King of All Britain.

It was because the King's grandfather, Alfred the Great, had had a love for learning, that choir schools had been established in the great abbeys and minsters throughout his domain, and that the Bishop of Winchester himself took a hand in teaching the boys their letters. The Bishop, like several of the teaching friars, was an Irish scholar who showed his affection for Waet by demanding that he do his lessons better than the other choir boys. And Waet grumbled because the Bishop bore down hard on him. But this only made Waet wiser and wittier and caused his fellow choristers to admire him all the more.

Waet knew that tonight after his meager supper would come compline and, because this was Nicholmas Eve, after compline the choir would assemble in the monastery kitchen to elect this year's Boy Bishop who would preside over the Christmas festivities. Waet had friends enough to win the election for himself, but he preferred, this year at least, to exert his influence over those friends to confer the honor onto the quiet and studious Dunstan.

Earlier in the year Dunstan had won the King's attention when he carried the King's mace in procession on Saint Swithin's Day and since then the royal favor had brought Dunstan special training as acolyte and deacon. This favoritism did not endear Dunstan to others in the church school, but Waet craftily worked to overcome prejudice against Dunstan. "The time will come," he often said in these quiet conversations with other students, "when Dunstan will win for us warmth and light." Besides, he had a warm, personal admiration for the big, blond, somewhat clumsy Dunstan.

A bell clanged its monotonous summons, calling monks and choir to the refectory. From their cells they hurried, choir boys and acolytes scurrying along dim corridors, down slippery stone steps, out into the raw cold of the cloisters where they tumbled to a halt to make way for a procession of the monks resident in the minster of Winchester. Hoods of their vestments were pulled low over their brows so that no face was visible except that of Brother Azifus, who led the column, his lantern casting eerie shadows on the vaulted ceiling of the half-open, half-enclosed passageway.

Huddled in the doorwell with Kevon of Cornwall, Waet held back his still-pushing fellows who could not see what caused the blocking of their passage. They grew quiet and the whisper of monks' sandals reached their ears.

Snow blowing from the open-arched side of the cloister had glazed over the stone floor, and as the boys fell into step behind the monks there was at first a cautious attempt at sure-footing, then a stumbling, tumbling attempt to slide over the glossy stones.

They filed into the warm, candlelit dining hall, suppressed whispers and laughter dying with the echoes of their footsteps. After a long chanted plea for God's blessing, the choristers and altar boys scrambled for their seats along the refectory tables. This was a joyous time of day, for the Bishop and monks allowed the young ones to chatter and jostle playfully, to enjoy a free and easy interplay over the evening meal that was permitted at no other time of day.

Tonight it was Kevon who tore apart the immense loaf of bread and distributed the chunks of crusty goodness to the boys at his table—smaller pieces to fatter boys, larger to his frailer, thinner fellows, "to make them grow." Habon of Wight, son of the ruler of that small kingdom, ladled a thick brown stew into heavy earthen bowls, while Waet poured a little watered wine into each cup. As they ate, the boys chattered of the fun they would have during the holidays ahead.

The monks, many of them young enough to recall their own happy days in the choir school, took pleasure in watching the boys turn the simple fare into a rollicking feast this Nicholmas Eve. At the end of the meal, the eternal bell tolled. As one, monks and students rose. They went in silent procession through the chapter house and into the stone-cold chapel. Candles in the shrines shivered in the air stirred by the moving bodies. When at last each flame stood still, the Bishop of Winchester pronounced a blessing, and the congregation solemnly recited the verses of compline, their thanks for a good day and their prayer for a calm and peaceful night.

Upon the Bishop's dismissal, the choir boys ran pell-mell from the chapel. In the monks' kitchen, Brother Azifus went over the rules for the election of the Boy Bishop. "You have need to remember the good deeds done by the candidate. You are under obligation to choose him whom you know to be kind and considerate of others—especially the brothers who carry out the menial tasks which contribute to the comfort of all."

"Ah-ha!" thought Waet, "Just what I have been telling everyone about Dunstan."

"For you never know," added Brother Azifus, "when the Boy Bishop can do kindnesses which will be turned toward you."

Under his breath, Kevon the Admiral's son muttered, "You mean, when the Boy Bishop can do things favoring Brother Azifus."

"Hist!" warned Waet. "If he heard you, he'd read you a homily on charity and respect." Waet looked round the kitchen and caught the eye of several of his friends. When they heard Brother Azifus say, "And now for the task before us. Who shall reign as Boy Bishop over the festival days of Christmas?", Waet gave them a nod as signal.

Immediately a hubbub of voices filled the kitchen. Kevon climbed up to stand on the bench where he and Waet had been sitting. "We want Dunstan to be our Bishop," the Admiral's son declared solemnly, "and none other. Dunstan possesses the spirit of Christmas, the sweet charity of Christ, and the dignity of Brother Azifus."

Kevon's oratory had the desired effect. The boys turned to look at Dunstan, who sat a little to one side, alone. Waet thought, "He's alone. He's always alone. I have never noticed how lonely he is." The hubbub rose again and Dunstan stood up, amazement flickering over his face. He colored, red blood flushing into his neck and cheeks.

Brother Azifus, not at all pleased with the way the situation was developing, wrung his hands and repeated over and over, "Are you sure, are you all in accord? Are you very sure?"

Waet, seeing Dunstan's discomfort and fearing he might decline the honor, scrambled to his side and laid a friendly arm over the young nobleman's shoulders. "We are sure, Brother Azifus, we are sure. We recognize in Dunstan the qualities needed for him to become an important churchman. He is steadfast in his devotion, he is meek, he is mild; he has won our respect." Waet hesitated, choosing his words carefully. Through his mind raced ideas of how Dunstan could turn the influence of his office as Boy Bishop into improvements in the lot of the choir boys and acolytes; he knew that the Boy Bishop had the power to do many things: grant dispensations, levy tax on the minster treasury, even demand services of the monks and friars who were bound to obey his commandments as though they were uttered by the Bishop himself.

At this moment, Kevon, having recognized Waet's signal, closed in on Brother Azifus. Kevon stood half a head taller than the round-headed, round-shouldered, round-bellied brown-clad monk. He could not be denied when he called for the vote to be taken. And the vote went emphatically in favor of Dunstan.

Kevon and Waet lifted the new Boy Bishop and in a trice he was standing above them all on a table. Reassured by the faces of the boys looking up to him, Dunstan spoke. "I will serve you as Bishop the best I can. And my first ceremonial act will be to dismiss all monks and clergy from this convocation, that I may hear the wishes freely expressed by my congregation."

The boys circled the long table and pounded it with their fists. "Decree! Decree!" they shouted. "Dismiss the clergy!"

Brother Azifus, prepared for this normal development in the reign of the Boy Bishop, solemnly signalled his brothers to follow him as he withdrew from the monks' kitchen. And when the boys felt that they were entirely alone, they made their wishes known to their Bishop Dunstan.

Over the din, Kevon bellowed, "Decree that we be instructed in the mathematic, Dunstan. I do not believe in the magic or evil of numbers. Mystical though they be, they can be useful to us in measuring land and building towers." He was shouted down by others demanding more food and drink than they were usually allowed by the monks.

"Fasting, fasting, always fasting," snarled several of the boys. "The friars do not fast as often as the choir." Dunstan listened, then turned to one who had remained quiet. "What say you, Waet?"

As he stood up, Waet ran his fingers through his rumpled hair. Out of the corner of his eye he saw a movement in the shadows beyond the cupboards. Again he felt the need to speak carefully. "What's been said about food and mead and mathematics is valid; these are but some of our needs. But we must remember that too many demands will put Dunstan out of favor with the Bishop and Brother Azifus. They will grant so many wishes, then nothing more."

Groans of disappointment rumbled in the kitchen. "Then what's the good?" scoffed Kevon. He kicked off his sandals and banged them together to loosen mud.

"There are other ways Dunstan can win us favors," Waet said clearly. And again he saw the stirring in the shadows. "I think we must tread lightly," he continued. "Dunstan must not be forced to pay too high a price to improve our lot. If we proceed slowly, many pleasant things will come to be."

Dunstan, the better to talk directly with his fellows, sat down on the table's edge. He searched the faces of those surrounding him. "Trust Waet and me. We will talk over every possibility and will tell you what we have decided before I press demands on the Bishop." He saw understanding and respect in the sea of eyes. "Go now," he said. "Return to your cells, as your Bishop commands you. We shall meet again tomorrow."

Reluctantly, the choir boys and acolytes shuffled from the warmth of the kitchen to their cold monastery cells. Dunstan stood up and stretched his arms, then rubbed his eyes. He shook his head to loosen neck muscles. "And now, Waet," he began.

"Hist!" Waet cautioned. "We are not alone."

"Of course you are not alone," boomed a voice. From the shadows between cupboards strode a tall, handsome man in leather suit and boots. Waet saw, standing within arm's reach, Athelstan, King of All Britain. Both boys dropped at once to one knee. After a moment, the king placed a hand on Dunstan's shoulder, and then on Waet's. "You are never alone, for your God is always with you, and sometimes, your king." He motioned for the boys to rise.

"It is not my custom to spy upon the affairs of schoolboys," said the king. "I was curious to see and study this survival of the ancient idea of democracy; it is an intriguing idea, this election of one from a group. I thought I saw it working."

"You are mistaken, Sire," replied Waet bluntly. "Dunstan was not chosen for his virtues. We merely traded on his power to do favors."

The king saw clearly Waet's cold belligerence for what it was—resentment at this interference in the boys' affairs. Yet he did not let it influence his reply. "It is you who are mistaken. Dunstan was chosen for those virtues because I chose him for them. And you chose him because he can persuade me to make situations favorable for you. That was sensible, and you have every reason to accept the favors graciously and in friendship."

Stunned by the king's adroit sidestepping of his rudeness, Waet stood silent as he heard Dunstan explain, "Though he has shown you little grace, Majesty, Waet is in every way a friend."

This reply pleased Athelstan. "That is good," he said. "We have need of friends, you and I." The king sat on a bench and pulled the candle close to his face, which now showed faint tracings of battle scars. "And we have need to tell our friend why the king has singled you out as someone special." He tugged on Waet's sleeve. "Come, sit. You must know certain things before you can believe."

Waet did as he was commanded, and watched the candlelight flicker in the king's eyes. "My Lord, " he stammered, "I am not of noble birth, as is Dunstan."

"Your loyal support will be required of you. If you cannot give it without question until you draw your last breath, speak now and I will let you go without troubling you further," The king spoke quietly, without hint of malice or prejudgment.

Waet's imagination raced through many possible explanations for the king's interest in two young students, but he was not prepared for the reason that unfolded.

"When I came to manhood," the king said simply, "it was found that I could never sire a child. This worried me not at all, since I was consumed with the glories of battle, driving the invaders north and out to sea. My father, Kind Eadward, remarried after my mother's death and provided other heirs to the throne. My brother Aelfweard was next in line, but he died only a month after my father's state funeral in January. That leaves Britain with two little boys as possible future kings: Eadmund, five years old and Eadred, four. Their mother, Queen Eadgifu, insists that I take them into my household and prepare them for the task of ruling All Britain." The king paused and looked away into the shadows.

"A heavy responsibility for a warrior king," muttered Dunstan. He felt he needed to reinforce the king's story to prepare Waet for what he must still hear.

A frown flickered over Athelstan's face. "I am in the process of moving the royal seat of government to Glastonbury where I can assemble a house of learned advisors. I have been so concerned with this move that I was not prepared for the Queen's stand. 'I have provided Britain with an heir and an heir presumptive,' she told me. 'You can expect no more from me.' Whereupon she packed her belongings and travelled north to live the rest of her life in a nunnery." Athelstan rubbed his bearded face with both hands before continuing.

"I am pleased to have the raising of my little brothers, but I cannot do it alone. That is why I have come to Winchester seeking scholars who can be trained to serve the little princes, first as companions but later as advisors in affairs spiritual and temporal."

The king continued his explanation. The Bishop of Winchester, the wise and scholarly Frithstan, had welcomed the king and readily agreed to help him in the search for suitable students who could be educated to serve as friends and advisors for two lonely little boys. He encouraged the king to come and go, dressed as one of the monks and therefore unrecognized, to observe the scholars as they took their lessons, did their assigned chores and followed the Cathedral school's routine. This suggestion Athelstan accepted, and from the choir members and acolytes he first chose Dunstan, whom the Bishop declared to be the most pious and dedicated of all candidates to the order of monks at the Cathedral.

Some of the cathedral school students had become jealous and suspicious of Dunstan when they learned he had won the king's favor. But both Bishop and king noted how Waet had used his influence with the other boys to save Dunstan greater embarrassment. And now the king sat facing the red-haired Celtic youth, explaining why he had been singled out as the second of the tutors for the little princes.

"We saw that everyone, boys and monks alike, admired your good sense and good humor," Athelstan continued. "if you can sway foreign dignitaries as smoothly as you do your schoolmates, you will perform great service for your king and for Britain. Therefore, I propose that you be given special tutoring in languages and diplomacy while Dunstan is prepared for ordination and the administration of church affairs. In this way both Eadmond, if he is to be king, and Eadred, if it falls his lot to rule, will grow up, knowing and depending upon their closest advisors and friends. You and Dunstan will live in the royal household at Glastonbury and continue your education with the learned professors in Glastonbury Abbey."

"Ah, Majesty—"said Waet uncertainly. "Your plan would lead to a fascinating career for me. But we have my father to reckon with. He has named me Waet, hoping that one day I will lead the Waetlings when, surely, they will rise again."

"I know your father well and have already won his approval for my proposition." The king rose from his seat and the boys scrambled to stand in his presence. "For the time, you will proceed with your life here at Winchester. Immediately after the Feast of the Epiphany you will be escorted to the palace in Glastonbury where your rank will be that of cousins to the little princes." Athelstan held out both his hands. Waet reluctantly grasped the right hand, a sign that he accepted the king's call to service.

Dunstan thumped Waet's shoulder and said joyfully, "Now we will study and work together for England."

The king untied the strings of his money pouch, selected three heavy gold coins and sent them spinning on the table top. "For the holiday feasting," he explained.

"But Sire," said Waet, "the monastery will provide the holiday feasts. What we need most is candles to study and work by, to provide us with light to do our tasks instead of those stinking pig-fat lamps."

Waet's bluntness amused Athelstan. "For candles, then," he said, and went off to take his leave of the Bishop of Winchester, satisfied that he had won an ally in Waet.

Waet was filled with doubts and asked himself, again and again, "Why me? Why have I been chosen to do this thing?" And years later, when he asked Bishop Dunstan this same question, Dunstan's answer was: "The hand of God traces a pattern on the wall of time. We follow the pattern, do God's will. We call it Fate, and when 'tis done, we call it History."

But for now, they were boys, happily anticipating their holidays and the joy of using the king's gold coins.

The following morning, Nicholmas Day, Dunstan appeared before Brother Azifus. "I am asking permission for Waet and me to go into the city. The king has given us money and we will go to the candlemaker's shop to buy candles."

A happy grin creased the round face of Brother Azifus. "How brightly lighted the shrines will be!"

"Our candles are not for the shrines," said Dunstan. "Each student of the Abbey school is to have two candles a week for study in his cell, a gift from King Athelstan. How long they will last will depend on how well we bargain with the chandler."

Brother Azifus beamed, and offered to do the purchasing, but the Boy Bishop was adamant and, reluctantly, Azifus granted the requested permission.

Dunstan and Waet hurried down the lane from the Abbott's close into the city streets and on into the marketplace. Winchester merchants bowed deferentially to the young men, recognizing them as students of the church school, all sons of wealthy families, certainly with money to spend and patronage to give. But they were not to be distracted by spices or trinkets or foreign delicacies. They made their way to the chandler's shop without delay.

Like most shops in the crafters' row, the candlemaker's was a three-sided affair, with the fourth side fastened at the top with leather hinges so that it could be raised and held up by poles to make an awning over the entrance to the work area. Cold as it was outside, Dunstan and Waet found the shop warm and inviting because the chandler had fires burning under cauldrons of melted tallow and beeswax. The air was heavy with the scent of sandalwood oil which told Dunstan that today candles were being made to be burned in the manor houses of wealthy citizens of Winchester.

The chandler was assisted by a young girl, his daughter, who tied wicks, evenly spaced, to wooden rods. Holding the rod at its midpoint, she dipped the wicks into a kettle of wax, raised the rod slowly, then set it in its own notch in the drying rack. Waet watched, fascinated, as she took an already dried set of slim candles to the next kettle and deftly gave the tapers another coating of wax. The girl held them in a draft of cooler air as they turned from a glossy shimmer to satiny smoothness. "We dip them sixteen times," she said as she returned the rod to the rack. "For the last four coatings, my father must dip and carry them, they get so heavy."

The chandler, inserting himself protectively between his daughter and the young noblemen, inquired about their business. As they discussed and bargained for the candles they wanted to buy, Waet and Dunstan earned respect from Kaffa the chandler, and he felt free to summon his daughter. "Ethel, bring samples for the customers to inspect."

From bins the girl selected candles of several lengths and thicknesses. As she delivered them into the hands of her father, he described each one. "This white is harder than the yellowish one. It will burn longer, but the flame will be less golden—less like the sun, more like the light of the moon."

Waet accepted a candle from the candlemaker's hand and held it to his nose, sniffing.

"These are scented with ferns gathered from marshy meadows," Ethel told him. "They are not so costly as sandalwood, yet they burn with a woodsy smell." Waet looked at the girl and she smiled cheerfully, as she would for any customer in the shop. It was a smile Waet would remember for years.

"How long will they burn?" asked Dunstan.

Kaffa rubbed his beard before replying. "In quiet air, two nights from sundown to sunrise; but in drafts, they flicker and gutter and are gone in a few hours." Waet thought of the snow that drifted through the cracks in his shutter and wondered, "If the cracks were filled with clay . . . ?" Fewer drafts, then.

Dunstan showed Kaffa the king's gold coins. "How many candles will these buy?" he asked.

Kaffa considered; he scratched on the back of his hand and mumbled a calculation as the two boys and the lovely girl waited his answer. "Three hundred twenty," he said finally.

"But since it is for the monastery," Ethel hastily added, "my father always gives extra measure. In this case, it would come to four hundred."

A storm brewed on Kaffa's face; he was about to explode when Ethel added, "Four hundred, even." Her smile told Dunstan and Waet that they had better learn a thing or two about dealing with tradesmen.

And they quickly put to work the lesson they had learned. They set about selecting the longest and straightest candles in the bins, while Kaffa grumbled that dealing with the monastery could drive a man to begging.

When the counting was complete, Waet and Dunstan found they could not carry away the merchandise and would have to come back the next day with a cart or a barrow to transport the candles to the church school. Ethel laughed at their predicament. Even her father was amused, and the boys went away admitting that the situation was, indeed, ridiculous.

On their way back to the minster, Waet suggested that they enlist several of their fellows in bringing the candles back to the school. Dunstan would not hear of it. "We must surprise every one with the king's gift," he said. "We can borrow a barrow from the Bishop's gardener, and throw some sacking over our treasure, so no one can guess what we have hidden." To this Waet agreed.

As it happened, snow covered the countryside that night, and it was several days before the two could venture down into the city again, this time wheeling a barrow through the streets and alleyways to the chandler's shop.

With many a sly jibe, Kaffa and Ethel loaded the candles onto the flat surface, heaping them into neat, even pyramids, then tying down the cover firmly, not only to keep prying eyes from discovering the contents, but, more important, to keep the load from shifting and rolling into the streets as Dunstan and Waet took turns trundling their treasure up to the minster. Once on home ground, the gardener (now an ally sworn to secrecy) helped them conceal candles and barrow in the grass barn.

Meanwhile, there were other matters to consider and in the following week Dunstan called for another convocation. "I have considered seriously Kevon's request that we be given instruction in mathematics," the Boy Bishop reported. "I have inquired into the matter and found that Brother Cowan has delved into these studies while he was in France. He has expressed a willingness to share with us the mysteries of numbers and what can be done with them, and the measurement of areas. Therefore I am preparing for the Bishop's approval a decree permitting any who wish such instruction to attend Brother Cowan's lectures. He will meet with us at the time we regularly have Latin Grammar lessons, his lectures to continue until the Feast of the Epiphany."

Shouts of approval met this announcement and it was some

time before the convocation could consider the next item of importance, the Nativity procession and pageant.

It was the custom, on the eve before Christmas Day, for the choir school to present a pageant relating the miracle of Christ's birth in the spacious Abbey church, to which the people of the parish were invited.

"Who is to be King Melchior?" asked Gunthar, who had taken that role last year. "And Balthazar?" demanded another.

Dunstan looked to Waet for support. Then, certain of his ground, the Boy Bishop stared the noisy ones down and said, "We will have the procession and the pageant, but I will not permit it to turn rowdy, as it has in some years past. You may have all the fun you want outside the church. Go dance in the stubbled fields, if that is your wish. As for the pageant, we will play out the miracle story with dignity."

Dunstan's reply subdued most of the mischief makers. But Ossian, older and apt to be more rebellious than the others, demanded to know "Who is to be Mary?" He had made a travesty of the role year before last, with his oglings and mimicking of pompous ladies, until the whole congregation was laughing and Brother Azifus had to step in and call a halt to the performance.

Sensing a challenge to Dunstan's authority, the boys grew tense and quiet. But Dunstan was not so easily to be drawn into battle. Instead, he said quietly, "In the city of Winchester there is a chandler whose daughter Ethel is as young and beautiful and innocent as the Blessed Mother was. It is my intention to ask her to be Mary in our procession and pageant."

Ossian scoffed. "No man will turn his daughter loose in a choir school." Here could be heard some chortles.

"That is true," admitted Dunstan. "Kaffa the chandler guards his daughter carefully and will continue to do so all the while he sits in the congregation watching his child portray the Blessed Mother. He will not allow Ethel to come within arm's reach of you, Ossian."

"It matters naught to me," sneered Ossian. "Bishop Frithstan has granted me leave to go to Wales with my lady-mother and her uncle while the rest of you stay here with your little games and petty feasts." He stormed out of the warm kitchen into the cold courtyard. Now he had done it, Ossian thought to himself as he stamped his feet and pounded the gate post with his fist. He did not want to go to Wales with his lady-mother and her uncle.

Bishop Frithstan had written them, asking them to remove Ossian from the choir school because of his defiance of rules. His lady-mother had sent a reply, begging Frithstan to give Ossian another trial period before expelling him. And the Bishop had relented, promising Ossian yet another chance—but now?

In a frenzy, he ran back to the kitchen door and flung it open, bellowing an insult: "King's favorite!"

Waet, closer to the door than any of the others, hurried out into the courtyard, closing the door quietly behind him. He reached Ossian, spun him around, and grasped him firmly while Ossian kicked and cursed and struggled to get free.

When Ossian grew calmer and violence fled, Waet released him. "We are all favorites of the king," he said quietly. "You will see. Presents will be given to all of us Christmas Eve in the name of King Athelstan."

After his outburst, Ossian was subdued, in despair. "I will receive none. When the bishop hears of this he will surely expel me."

"He will not hear of it from me, nor from Dunstan."

"There are devils in me that have their way, and I must do their bidding."

"Do not blame devils for your bad temper and willfulness. They are yours, and you alone can curb them. If I were you, I would go to Bishop Frithstan and tell him of this incident, and ask him to help you overcome your difficulty."

Ossian's temper flared up, and he raised his fist to strike. When he saw that Waet would not fight him, he withdrew his hand. He said simply, " I will do that."

From the kitchen door Dunstan and several other boys

watched as Ossian turned away and fled toward the Bishop's apartments. They were quiet, subdued by what they had seen.

Waet worked hard to revive happy anticipation in planning for the coming festivities. "Who is willing to braid the bread?" he asked, and when that was settled he found volunteers to take on the tasks of stoning the dried plums and separating the membrane from the suet for the boiled puddings. Christmas Eve was now only a week away. Each one went happily and willingly to his tasks.

With the wintry sun sending slanted rays their way, Dunstan and Waet went down into the marketplace to ask Kaffa to permit his daughter Ethel to come to the cathedral to portray the Virgin Mother in the pageant. To their surprise, Kaffa welcomed the proposal. Though Ethel blushed at being compared with Christ's mother, she too was pleased. She learned readily what she must do and say during the pageant. While the young people rehearsed the speeches, Kaffa thought how good it would be for his business to brag to other merchants that he was invited to the Abbey expressly to bring his own Ethel to portray the Virgin Mary in the miracle play. The time of their arrival at the Abbey on Christmas Eve was agreed upon, and Kaffa pressed a costly taper into Dunstan's hand. "Burn it in Mary's shrine, a prayer that the pageant may go well."

Waet and Dunstan, satisfied that their plans were falling into place nicely, went back to the monastery, now busy with preparations for the holy feast day.

In the week that followed, Waet saw little of Ossian, and then only at a distance. Only once did he notice that Ossian sat tying knots in a long thick rope. He was too busy to wonder at the sight of the ill-tempered one, silently pulling the rope through still another loop.

Into the storerooms and pantries great quantities of supplies poured, some from reserve barns in distant fields belonging to the Abbey, and some from the households of landed gentry. The bake house and kitchen were kept busy for long hours and on the morning before Christmas Eve, a company of the king's foot soldiers brought in a fine fresh-killed stag. Brother Azifus put on a leather butcher's apron and cut the stag into sections fit for roasting on the spit. "Christmas is such a busy time," panted Brother Azifus, but neither he nor anyone else begrudged the extra effort.

All parts for the pageant had been assigned, the choir and acolytes practicing steadily until Dunstan and Waet believed it would go smoothly Christmas Eve. And still no trouble from Ossian, who sat in a corner untying the knots of his rope and then methodically tying them again with occasional variations in the types of knots he used.

The afternoon of Christmas Eve flew by. Waet had sorted out the costumes acquired by the choir school over the years, castoffs from the wealthy relatives of students. Now he had them all laid out in place for each player—even the rich red velvet robe to be worn by the chandler's daughter as Mary.

Just at sunset, Kaffa arrived at the Abbey gate with his daughter Ethel. Dunstan led them to the monks' kitchen where they were fed, along with the other players, an early meal. As had been predicted, Kaffa did not let Ethel out of his sight until Waet led him to a prominent seat in the Abbey church. As other citizens of Winchester began assembling around him, Kaffa introduced himself and proudly announced that he was the father of the Virgin Mary. Without doubt, he was having an enjoyable visit.

To the rear of the church, Waet distributed the costumes while Dunstan lined up Mary and Joseph, the Angel of the Annunciation, the shepherds and the wise kings from afar, all the while refreshing the memories of those who had forgotten their speeches. Kevon of Cornwall shivered in his gauzy attire as the Angel; he wished for heavier undergarments, but nothing had been found that would not show through the filmy material. Mary shone with a rare beauty in her red velvet, and all was in readiness for the procession to begin.

A lively fanfare rippled from brass trumpets, and the choir sang a "Gloria, gloria, in excelsis Deo" to the congregation which now filled the church. Majestically, the procession flowed down the center aisle, and the pageant began to unfold.

"Hail, thou that art highly favored," sang out Kevon in a clear, angelic voice. "The Lord is with thee; blessed art thou among women."

Ethel, radiant in her red velvet, pressed a hand to her shoulder, turning from one side to the other, showing everyone a troubled face.

"Fear not, Mary, for thou hast found favor with God," proclaimed the angel. "And behold, thou shalt conceive and bring forth a son and shalt call his name Jesus." And it seemed as though Kevon was indeed the Angel of the Annunciation, for his raiment shimmered in the candle light and his voice climbed to the arches of the cathedral ceiling.

Mary, all modest and simple, asked, "How shall this be, seeing I know not a man?"

Again the voice from the ages mystified every listener. "The Holy Ghost shall come upon thee, and the power of the highest shall overshadow thee."

Mary bowed low to the angel, touching her forehead to her knee. "Behold the handmaid of the Lord," said she. "Be it unto me, according to thy word." The beautiful young girl raised her head and stepped forward. It was as though her heart sang with the words she spoke. "My soul doth magnify the Lord and my spirit hath rejoiced in God my Savior." A sigh caught in her throat, then Ethel went on triumphantly. "Behold, from henceforth all generations shall call me blessed."

"Ohs" and "Ahs" broke the spell, and the pageant proceeded.

"Joseph went up from Galilee to be taxed with Mary his espoused wife, being great with child. And so it was that, while they were there, the days were accomplished that she should be delivered . . ."

Silently, a stable of wood and a manger filled with straw

glided into the nave of the church, and Mary bowed her head and knelt beside the manger.

"And she brought forth her firstborn son and laid him in a manger because there was no room for them in the inn . . ." Mary's hands were in the straw of the manger, fondling her baby, Jesus.

From the choir came five boys in shabby cloaks, making their way toward the manger.

"And there were in the same country shepherds abiding in the field, keeping watch over their flock at night. And lo, the angel of the Lord came upon them and they were sore afraid . . ." Again, Kevon's voice rang clear: "I bring you glad tidings. For unto you is born this day a Savior which is Christ the Lord."

Never had shepherds rejoiced more happily, never had three resplendently attired kings been more majestic. And never had the students of Winchester's Choir School any greater pleasure than they had in performing their miracle play.

When at last the pageant drew to its close, Dunstan signalled for Waet and Gunthar to trundle in the barrow full of candles. "These are King Athelstan's gift to the students of our school. There will be two candles a week for each of you to use in your cells, until the supply is gone. Then perhaps the good friars and our Bishop will continue to provide them when they see how your work is improved when it is done under better light." With this, Dunstan began to distribute the candles as the boys came forward to receive them. Waet, seeing Ossian hanging back, urged him to go up to receive his gift from the king. Ossian laid down his knotted rope, claimed his two candles, then returned to Waet's side.

"The Bishop is helping me curb my willfulness," Ossian said. "When I am angry, I tie harder knots; untying hard knots is painful and difficult and I can forget what I was angry about. The Bishop taught me. He says that in time I may not need the rope."

When the service was over, Dunstan and Waet obtained permission from Brother Azifus to walk Ethel and her father to their home in the city. Every step of the way Kaffa bubbled and boasted so much that the young people had little chance to talk to each other. Yet Waet and Dunstan knew that Ethel would never forget the night she became the Blessed Mother for their pageant.

On their way back to the Abbey Dunstan said, "We're not boys any longer, Waet. Soon we will have to assume the serious work of helping the little princes get ready to be kings."

"I had forgotten," admitted Waet. "And between now and the Feast of the Epiphany you must try to forget too. Time enough then to assume responsibility for matters spiritual and temporal."

Beyond the Castle Wall

France—The Second Crusade

Crellon, pretending the carpenter's horse was a sleek, black steed, kicked his heels against its legs and crowed, "When I grow big, I shall be a great horseman, and ride off to the Crusades to save the Holy Land from the Terrible Turks!"

His sister Valerie tugged on his scarf. "No, you shall not go," she said, "unless you take me!" and she gave the scarf another pull.

Crellon's legs were longer than those of the wooden sawhorse. Valerie's second tug almost made him lose his seat. "But girls can't go on Crusades," he protested.

"Yes, they can," insisted Valerie. "They can if their brothers take them. Oh, take me along, Crellon! I shall disguise myself as your faithful page."

"My horseboy," Crellon teased.

"As your tireless and ever-faithful horseboy," Valerie agreed. "And I'll follow you to the gates of Jerusalem—."

Crellon broke in again: "First to the gates of Constantinople, to wipe out the shadow of the non-believers."

Another sister, Madeleine, who had been quietly knitting as she stood watching the younger children playing, tried to correct Crellon by saying, "No! They call *us* non-believers, Bordolaire tells me." Madeleine was two years older than her brother and was quite certain she understood world affairs much better than he.

But Crellon only scoffed. "Doesn't matter. We shall have to storm Constantinople before we can free the Holy Land."

Valerie turned to Madeleine and asked, "But won't the Turks stop Crellon before he gets any where near Constantinople?"

The smile Madeleine wore faded. "Who's to know?" she replied. "It's said that Turks are everywhere these days. But here in France, how can we know? Constantinople is half a world away."

"Then I must go half way round the world," said Crellon, "and then you'll see whether or not I conquer the Turkish capital."

Valerie hopped up onto the wooden horse behind her brother. "Turks won't let you," she said, "unless you have me to bargain for your head, like Lady Charlotte in the ballad."

These were the children of the Duc de Bresserie, all three showing signs of having played in the muddiest part of the courtyard of the great castle. Already the sun had gone down beyond the towers and slitted parapets atop the castle wall, casting their shadows on the massive stone stairs winding round the turret bases that made up the opposite wall of the courtyard.

The heavy wooden door to the kitchen swung open. A long arm with pointing finger came into view, followed by the head and shoulders of Bordolaire, matron of the Duc's kitchen. "Come out of the mud, you naughty children," she scolded. "You must have your supper before your father, the Duc, will be satisfied to sit down to eat his."

The boy and his sisters abandoned their play, walked to the entrance, and scraped their shoes over the edge of the stone step before tumbling into Bordolaire's warm, steaming kitchen.

"Off with those dirty cloaks!" Bordolaire screeched. "And the shoes, too. Drop them in the corner and you can clean them when they dry. There's not much water, but enough for you to wash your hands. I keep praying for the spring rains to begin!"

Madeleine hung her cloak on a peg beside the door and set her shoes neatly in the corner. She turned, smiling, to Bordolaire. "When the rains come, the courtyard grass will grow, and we won't get dirty."

Little Valerie came skipping to the bench beside the kitchen table; she sat down and swung her stockinged feet up onto the seat. "But then we can have a garden, if Papa will permit it, and we can play in the dirt all day, with no one to scold us."

"There will be plenty of water for washing as well as for sprinkling your garden!" snapped Bordolaire.

Crellon brought the basin of water from the cupboard to the table. He smiled, thinking of the spring rain. "Then the moat will be filled," he thought, "and I can swim in it."

Bordolaire brought a towel for drying their hands. As she carried away the wash-water, she said, "When the time comes, I will have you out from under foot, and I will be able to keep my kitchen clean. Come, sit up; your supper's waiting."

As they took their seats at the table, Crellon asked, "When will you bake the meat in a pie again? That I like, Bordolaire."

Bordolaire had to fight hard to keep from showing her fondness for Crellon. She would have promised to make him a meat pie the very next day, but no—that would be spoiling him. Instead, she said, "When your mother, the Duchesse, tells me to, and not before. Now, eat what's in front of you and I'll let you go sit on the stairs in the great hall."

"Why?" asked Madeleine. "Is something interesting happening?"

Bordolaire considered for a moment, then told them, "Well, it's said that the King of France comes here tonight to enlist your father in the Crusade." And as she saw Valerie's face begin to crinkle, she added, "Now, now, Valerie, no need to cry."

"But I don't want Papa to go!" Valerie wailed. "Madeleine said Constantinople is halfway round the world!"

Bordolaire would rather bite her tongue than say anything to disturb the Duc's children, but now that she had stumbled into this situation, she did her best to soothe the little one. "So it is, lamb, so it is. But no one believes that your Papa will go, even if the King asks him. Oh, he'll possibly send a score of men along, just to carry the banner of Chateau Bresserie. But, there! it isn't for us in the little kitchen to make decisions. That's for the fine ones in the great hall. And now you had better eat your supper, while I go help the other servants. With the King of France and his retinue to feed, they will be at their wits' end."

The kitchen was very quiet as Bordolaire tied a fresh apron around her waist. Crellon and Madeleine ate slowly, hoping Valerie had been talked out of her tears. When she saw that Bordolaire was ready to leave them, Madeleine said, "Before you go, may I take something to Madame Fredôme to eat? She will be afraid to come to the great hall if there are many strangers."

"Eh, Madeleine, you want to feed La Chatte?" Bordolaire turned to the cupboard and lifted out a dish. "I don't know why your mother permits that madwoman to roam at will through the castle. Here, she will like this piece of breast, and bread and cheese."

Madeleine left the table to take the plate from Bordolaire's hand. "Oh, thank you. Madame will be very grateful."

"Someday, she will repay our kindness by doing something terrible. Then I'll say I told you so." The kitchen matron turned on her heel and was about to mount the stone stairs to the great hall above when a bell was heard.

Crellon hopped up. "Hist!" he said. "I hear the drawbridge bell. Do you think the King has come already?"

Valerie pushed past him to the little window. "Here's Mama, coming across the courtyard. Help me swing open the door for her, Crellon!" The little girl bounced with excitement as the door swung back on creaky hinges to admit the beautiful Duchesse de Bresserie.

"Ah, here you are, my darlings," said the Duchesse over the murmur of silks as she removed her fur-lined walking cloak.

"Is it the King , Mama, is it the King?" bubbled Valerie.

The Duchesse patted the little one's cheek. "No, my Valerie, not yet. Your uncle, Le Compte Chandoore, was summoned by your Papa this morning, so I imagine it is he at the castle gate."

Madeleine, remembering hearing her father's account of his unpleasant and uncomfortable encounters with her Uncle Chandoore, wrinkled her face in distaste. True, she had never come face-to-face with the knight, and he was famous throughout France for his prowess in both jousts and dueling with swords. Still, whenever le Compte Chandoore was mentioned, Madeleine imagined him to be an ominous and dreadful figure.

The Duchesse, noting Madelaine's response, continued brightly. "A runner came some time ago to say that His Majesty is only two or three hours away. So there will be much excitement for you to see. It isn't every day that the King comes to Chateau Bresserie."

Bordolaire tried to explain the plate in Madeleine's hand. "Madeleine is going to take some food to Madame Fredôme, if Your Highness will permit it."

"Oh, yes, it's perfectly all right," said the Duchesse. She draped her cloak over her arm. "It would be better if Madame does not encounter the King. He may not understand her infirmity." The children watched their lovely mother walk toward the stairs. "There is so much to do!" She stopped and turned, considering. "When the children have finished their supper, Bordolaire, come to me in the great hall, and bring all the candles you can find. If we could only brighten the castle a little!" With a little sigh of discontent, the Duchesse hurried up the stairs.

Meanwhile, in a specially prepared withdrawing room, Roland, Duc de Bresserie, was welcoming his half-brother, Le Compte Chandoore. "Come, make your self comfortable, Chandoore," urged the Duc. "It has been a long time since we've had a word together."

Chandoore, studying the Duc with dark eyes set deep in a dark face, agreed in a dark voice. "It has, indeed, been a long time since we stood together under our father's roof. I trust fortune has smiled upon you?"

The Duc shifted uneasily, recalling how unpleasant the parting of the half-brothers had been, long years ago. When your mother dies while you are an infant and your father goes off on a Crusade within two years, you are ill-prepared to accept the Turkish stepmother, princess though she be, whom your father brings back to you. Mirizshah, having a son of her own, made no pretense of caring for Roland. Therefore, his childhood had been sad and lonely until he went into service as squire to his father's friend, Le Duc Montblanc.

Then followed happy years for him as squire and knight. Roland was almost able to forget his unhappiness as a child, until he was summoned home on the occasion of the old Duc's death. His father had provided handsomely for the Princess Mirizshah and her son, Chandoore; but he had named Roland heir to Chateau Bresserie and the title. His stepmother fought furiously to gain title and castle for Chandoore; nevertheless, the old Duc's will withstood all legal assaults. The storming stepmother left the castle in a rage, and the half-brothers parted with bitter words on their lips.

Now, fourteen years later, all this must be set aside and Roland, Duc de Bresserie, must ask a favor of the man who thought he had every right to hate him. "I can no longer put off the demands of King Philip Augustus," he explained uneasily, "that I go with him on the next Crusade. I have told the King my family needs me, but he replies that he and the Cross need me more. So I ask you now, as my closest kinsman, to take my place as head of this household, while I accompany His Majesty to the Holy Land."

Chandoore, noting the Duc's discomfort, hid a smirk of satisfaction and replied only, "You honor me, dear brother."

The Duc felt immensely relieved by this apparent willingness of his half-brother to forget past unpleasantness. "I hoped you would favor me in this way," he said. "The Duchesse will be happy to have you take charge of Chateau Bresserie, in token whereof, I surrender to you my keys." The Duc unfastened the clasp holding the key ring to his belt; the keys, striking against each other, chimed as they were passed from hand to hand.

Chandoore, thinking how happily he would report this touching ceremony to his still-vindictive mother, murmured, "It is my good fortune to be of service to my kinsman."

The Duc, gratified that they had so easily set the past behind them, led his brother away to establish him in suitable accommodations. When he had made certain that Chandoore was settled comfortably, the Duc hurried to the great hall to inform the Duchesse of this new development.

The Duchesse was dismayed when she began to realize what Chandoore's presence meant. "Then you are going! Leaving me and our children to the tender mercies of Chandoore, a knight you have never trusted? Why, he's hardly ever been spoken of here, let alone welcome!"

The Duc tried to calm his Duchesse's fears. "Times are different, Mesaline. Three or four times I have put off the King, and I cannot do that any longer. Nor can I go off to the Crusades, leaving you unprotected."

"Why? Tell me why!"

The Duc sighed unhappily. It was so hard to explain that he would rather stay but that his own wishes must be set aside. He tried. "Because this time the King intends to go himself, and he has commanded me to go with him. I cannot refuse him and there is only Chandoore to call upon."

Biting back tears, the Duchesse snapped, "Then heaven help us and the children!" and returned to her chore of laying trenchers and napkins on the banquet table.

When they had finished eating their supper, Madeleine and Crellon descended to the underground storerooms where Madame Fredôme hid. Keeping well out of the shadows, Madeleine followed closely the candle Crellon carried. "It's scary in here," she said. "I don't see why Madame Fredôme likes being here."

Crellon scoffed. "Then why do you come? Do you like being scared?" This Madeleine denied and Crellon tried to reassure her. "I like being here, among the old pieces of armor and the ancient furniture. Some of it has been here for many hundred years—four or five hundred, anyway. See this strange chair, made of cross pieces? Abbé Frobein calls it a cathedra, and I have no doubt Madame Fredôme sits in it often." Crellon sat down in the cathedra himself.

Seeing this, Madeleine felt a little more at ease. "Last time I was here, Madame told me she especially likes the dungeon, and the water trickling from the moat." She set the plate of food for Madame on a little table.

"But there won't be any water trickling from the moat until the spring rains come to fill it," Crellon replied. Then, after a moment's silent waiting, he asked, "Well, what shall we do? Call for La Chatte, or leave her supper where she can find it?"

"Silly!" said Madeleine. "She knows we are here. Am I right, Madame?" She turned to peer into the shadows.

"You can't trick her like that!" scoffed Crellon.

But the voice of Madame Fredôme, with its varying pitches and harsh singing tones, came curling out of the darkness, "Oh, yes she can. My little lady Madeleine can trick me anytime. I like to be tricked." Now La Chatte crept stealthily from the shadows and stood there in her crackled leather slippers, her tattered red velvet dress and her halo of white, wispy hair. Her face was strangely beautiful and horrible. "I like being tricked, here among the ancient armor and furniture, just like you do."

Her words astounded Crellon. "You have heard everything we have said since we came down the stairs."

"And more, much more, dear boy," boasted Madame Fredôme. "I like to crawl up between the walls. You see, there is the scaffolding between the stone walls and the wood panels that make up the rooms and chambers, and holds up their floors. I am not called 'La Chatte' for nothing! Why, for every room there are four walls, and I may listen where and when I please. I know your Uncle Chandoore has come, and the King is yet to come. It is better if I do not encounter the King!" And she gave herself over to enjoying an all-knowing laugh.

Crellon broke in harshly, saying, "Hush! You are frightening Madeleine!"

But La Chatte merely twisted round and purred, "Am I? Dear Crellon, I think I am frightening you, but you think it more gallant to worry about the fears of my lady Madeleine." She danced into the shadows and her voice trailed after her. "Do I know what I know?"

There was a long, silent moment before they knew that La Chatte had gone. Madeleine shuddered and Crellon said hoarsely, "Come away, Madeleine. Poor Madame Fredôme is no better today."

Within the hour, la Duchesse and Bordolaire had lighted clusters of candles and, to please his Mesaline, the Duc had called for pitch-knot torches to be placed in iron wall brackets, augmenting the golden glow of the candles. Beautifully dressed ladies and their handsomely caparisoned knights began assembling in the great hall to wait for the arrival of the King of France. They gathered in groups, laughed, and told each other their adventures of the day, for they were accustomed to being summoned, then having to wait.

Madeleine and Crellon and Valerie sat at the top of the great staircase, looking down upon the shifting pattern of the colorful company in the great hall. "See," said Valerie, "Mama is wearing her cloth-of-gold gown and it catches the light from the torches and tapers. The King will think she is the prettiest Duchesse in the whole of France."

"Most certainly," agreed Madeleine, and she was about to comment on her papa's green velvet doublet with silver breast plate when everyone in the great hall was startled by a voice crying out "The King of France comes!"

A young lad, Crellon's age, strode into the center of the hall where the Duc stood among his knights. "The King has sent me to announce him!"

"It's Jacques!" whispered Crellon to his sisters. "Messenger for the King, and only yesterday the son of a weaver."

Now the Duc stood facing the weaver's son. "Jacques

Portraine, what is this all about?"

"Truly, sire," replied Jacques, "the King stopped at our cottage, alone and unattended. He has persuaded my father to give up weaving and devote himself to the Crusade."

Le Compte Chandoore, who stood nearby, sneered at what he heard. "This seems strange behavior for a king, good brother Bresserie."

The Duc, immediately angered by his half-brother's comment, nevertheless softened his reply. "We have a strange and mystical King, but still, he is the King of France." He turned again to the weaver's son. "And where is the King now?"

Jacques has just time to reply, "His Majesty stands at the portcullis, waiting to be welcomed." A shaggy-headed, leather-clad figure strode into the circle of light.

"Waiting no longer!" thundered the man with glowing eyes, as gasps of dismay escaped the knights and ladies. They bowed and curtsied and breathed "Your Majesty" with customary awe. The King angrily waved them out of his way and demanded, "Know you not that I must be about my business?"

The Duc was too startled to stand on ceremony and ventured, "But, great King, alone? Unattended?"

His Majesty, like a great stone rolling downhill, plowed through the company toward the raised dais at the far end of the hall. "I have sent everyone in my retinue on ahead," he explained. "And I will go like a mendicant from castle to castle to rouse the lords and dukes in this great cause." But now he faltered and, recognizing his host and hostess, he softened his tone. "I bid you sup, for I have broken bread with a weaver who will weave no more."

The Duc de Bresserie was at a loss for words, but his Duchesse swept into a ceremonial curtsy and rising, placed her hand on His Majesty's arm. "You are welcome to Chateau Bresserie, beloved King. Come, you will sit with us, will you not?" Gracefully, she ushered the now-docile mendicant King to the throne prepared for him at the banquet table. In a moment, she gave a signal for the whole company to sit and dine.

"Now," said the King to the Duc and Duchesse, and to everyone else within hearing distance, "I can tell you of my great plans. Frederick Barbarossa is already on his way to Asia Minor with my blessing, and I am directing every available Frenchman to the Mediteranean where we will assemble for the march on Saladin's territory. Constantinople has been won and lost several times."

"Who occupies it now?" asked the Duc eagerly.

The King's face twisted in agony as he admitted, "I do not know. But we will have to take it, if it is not already ours." He turned to the beautiful Mesaline and begged, "Duchesse, I need your husband, and every knight and squire you can spare." And his glowing eyes stared far over the heads of the company before him.

The Duc, signaling Mesaline that she must not plead with the King, spoke his assurance: "I am ready, Sire. My brother, le Compte Chandoore, will head my household while I am gone."

"Then," responded the King, " you can not leave too soon. Tomorrow morning, or even tonight. Even a day may make the difference between success and failure."

The Duchesse, startled, rose and stood uncertainly at the King's elbow. "But, surely, you will stay the night?"

The King, seeming to wake from a trance, smiled and assured her. "Yes, my dear Duchessse. I will rest my head in Chateau Bresserie. But I must be up and away early. There are other landed gentry, not so ready to serve in the great cause as your husband, and I must impress them with their obligation to God. Best be a brave Duchesse and your Roland will return when the battle is won." The King turned his head wearily toward the Duc.

"I can feed and caparison only fifty-two knights and squires, Your Majesty."

The King put his hand on Roland's shoulder. "If they be willing soldiers, they will fight like two hundred. If they be earnest and inspired, they will be worth two thousand."

Le Compte Chandoore, insinuating his cynical comment,

asked, "And if they are not, Your Majesty?"

The King looked blankly into Chandoore's face and, when finally he recognized the doubter, he shook his head sadly. "We must not think of that. Saladin's men are swift and fierce executioners."

Chandoore could not hold back another barb, "So I have heard, Majesty."

The King rose, towering over his tormentor; without further comment he allowed the Duchesse to lead him to his bed chamber.

When morning came and the Duchesse was descending from her private quarters, she encountered, at the foot of the grand staircase, Chandoore, now keeper of the castle keys. "And how has the King slept?" she asked brightly.

Chandoore, suave and smooth, answered her just as brightly. "Very well, dear sister. His Majesty roused me early and, warning me not to disturb you, set out without breakfast, saying he could be many miles on his way before the sun climbs high."

The Duchesse allowed a tear to creep slowly down her cheek. "How good of him. He knows it's hard to tear a man away from his family." Feeling grateful that she could express her sadness to Chandoore, the Duchesse allowed herself to weep openly. "Now all too soon, my husband will come down the stairs and ride far away, beyond the castle wall, to the Mediterranean and thence to the Holy Land, in the King's service."

Chandoore made an effort to console her. "I will do my best to ease your burden, sister; but I fear it will be a long and hard campaign. Come, dry your tears. Put on a brave face for your lord and master as he rides forth."

Mesaline dried her tears and sighed. "I will call the children to bid farewell to their father."

But when she climbed the stairs, she found all three children having a rollicking time with their father in the Duc's dressing room.

"And who will lace your boots for you tomorrow?"

demanded Valerie who, plain to see, had been doing that service at the moment.

"One of the squires," replied the Duc. "Unless, of course, the King has other duties for him to perform."

"The King has left word with LeCompte Chandoore that he has other noblemen to recruit and that you are to proceed to Nice, where he will rejoin you." The Duchesse tried to make her message lighthearted and matter-of-fact, but the Duc heard the sadness creeping through her voice.

"Now I want you to go down to your breakfast," he told the children. "I need to have a few quiet moments with your mother." And when the young ones had gone, he added, "Please, Mesaline, no tears. I want to think of you always with a smile on your lips."

"I've done with tears, Roland. But I do wish you were twins; how gladly I would send one of you off to do battle for the King and Christianity if I had the other to stay at my side."

Roland kissed her gently. "I have tried to give you that by sending for Chandoore."

"Ah," sighed Mesaline, "but the difference between you is as great as night and day."

When the family had assembled in the great hall and were walking together to the courtyard, the Duc said, "And now, my dear daughters and son, I leave you in good hands. Your Uncle Chandoore will act in my stead. To him you owe obedience and respect. He and your mother will decide what is best for you while I am away on the Crusade. Do good, and I will be proud of you."

Madeleine hugged her papa and, looking up into his face, promised, "You will be proud of us, Papa."

Turning to his son, the Duc asked, "And you, Crellon?"

The boy hung back, hesitating, then rushed to his father and threw his arms around him. "I wish I were going with you, Papa." The Duc returned the hug, saying, "Another time, my son. You will have a chance to earn your armor, I promise you."

Valerie hopped up and down until the Duc picked her up in

his arms. "Oh, Papa, can't I go along with you and be your horseboy, like I'm going to be for Crellon some day? I'd be a tireless and ever faithful horseboy!"

But the Duc set her down, laughing and saying, "I forbid you to be a boy. I want you to be a lady, a princess who will turn every knight's head."

The trumpets sounded the call to horse and the Crusaders of Chateau Bresserie mounted their steeds. The Duc and his knights and squires rode off, their breastplates reflecting the morning sun.

The days and weeks that followed were long and lonely for the Duchesse and her children, especially for Crellon. His Uncle Chandoore's manner turned stern and distant; the men Chandoore brought with him and added to the castle guard were far from friendly.

One sunny afternoon, Crellon stood on the parapet. Looking down into the courtyard, he saw the guardsmen exercising a pair of young, lean dogs, new to the castle kennel. The boy hurried down the stone stairs built into the tower wall and ran toward the handsome animals. As he approached, both dogs snarled and bared their teeth. One of the guardsmen shouted, "Stand still, young master!" And just in time, for the dogs raced to him and, snarling viciously, circled round him until the guardsman had put leashes on them and taken them away.

"You will never approach those dogs without my permitting it," shouted the guardsman.

Crellon, frightened, explained, "I wanted only to pet them."

"They are guard dogs, trained to attack, and are never to be petted. You would be wise to remember that, young master." The man's tone warned Crellon that life in Chateau Bresserie was changing under Le Compte Chandoore's stewardship. And when he gave an account of the incident to his mother, she too admitted feeling that restrictions on the family's activities were slowly tightening.

As spring wore on, Crellon turned for friendship to Jacques Portraine, son of the weaver who would weave no more. One sunny day after the rains had filled the moat and brought up the marsh grasses on its banks, the two boys sat on the drawbridge in the warm sun.

"Come on, Jacques," Crellon suggested. "We'll swim in the moat."

The idea of a swim interested Jacques. "But the stream in the valley would be better. There are no mosquitoes."

"My uncle wouldn't permit it," said Crellon regretfully. "The moat is as far as I can go outside the walls."

Jacques made a face. "I see there are a lot of new guards on duty at the castle."

"Yes. They look like cutthroats to me, but they are loyal to my uncle."

"Have you had any word from your father, the Duc?"

"A runner came late yesterday. The whole army is assembled at Nice, waiting for the King. Do you wish your father had stayed at home, weaving?" Crellon had been expecting Jacques to ask him a similar question.

"No," sighed Jacques. "Each of us must do what his conscience drives him to do. But I wish you could come stay with me tonight. My mother is away, caring for a sick relative. Wouldn't you like to sleep in a cottage for once?"

Crellon shook his head. "I suppose you grow weary of hearing me repeat 'My Uncle Chandoore will say no.' But—" and here Crellon had a happy thought—"Why don't you stay the night with us in the castle? That I could arrange."

"All right," agreed Jacques. "Are you sure the Duchesse will not mind?"

Crellon was on his feet. "Come, we'll ask," he urged. "We can swim another day."

The Duchesse was pleased to break the monotony of her son's confinement to the castle. She herself was aware of the restraint imposed on her and her family by Le Compte Chandoore. "Oh, yes," she thought, "it's all done in the name of good management, or our personal safety. The children may not play in the courtyard because Chandoore's gardeners have planted there a formal garden of his Eastern herbs and shrubs. The ladies in waiting and I are denied dining in the great hall because the candles to light it are too costly. All must be sacrificed to keep sending supplies to the army. I shall have a choice bit of comment for the ears of the King of France when next I see him. Him and his Crusade!"

That evening after sunset, Jacques Portraine took supper with Crellon, Madeleine and Valerie.

"And in the village," said Jacques over his bowl of stew, "'tis said that Chateau Bresserie is haunted."

"Really?" Madeleine was amused. She asked, "And are the villagers frightened by these ghost stories?"

"I believe so, my lady. Are you frightened by them?"

"No, of certainty. I can't believe in ghosts."

As though to challenge Madeleine's denial of ghosts, there came from the panelled walls the sounds of three sharp knocks. Jacques was startled. "What can that be?" he asked in awe.

Now they heard the mournful, muffled chant of La Chatte. "The King of France would wish to dance, but now he languishes in chains. He hasn't seen the light of day since coming of spring rains."

Jacques' eyes opened wide with terror. "The voice comes from the wall. Surely you heard it as well as I?"

"Certainly," said Crellon.

"And you are not afraid?"

"No, no," declared Valerie. "That was no spirit, Jacques," she explained. "We have living in the castle an old, old woman, Madame Fredôme. The servants call her La Chatte — the cat— because, well—she just *is* the cat."

Madeleine took over the explanation of the mysterious voice behind the panels. "Madame has always lived in the castle, as long as Papa can remember. 'Tis said her husband, the great commander André Fredôme, who served under King Louis the Seventh, was lost in an earlier Crusade. When Madame learned this, she lost her wits and has been demented ever since."

"She is harmless, Jacques," added Valerie. "Madeleine takes her things to eat."

Jacques began to feel more at ease, accepting these reassurances. Still, his comment was: "Your castle is too much for me. I could never get used to it." He got up from the table and walked to the window.

Crellon was concerned that his friend would insist on going home."Oh, stay, Jacques," he coaxed. "Madame will not harm you, or even frighten you again."

"Think what fun it will be," Madeleine teased, "to tell the villagers that you heard our famous ghost."

Jacques allowed himself to be convinced by this clever suggestion, and so he stayed. When they were bedded down for the night in Crellon's chamber, the two boys talked long of the day when they themselves would ride forth as knights on a pilgrimage. At last, sleep overtook them. But at a cold, dark hour during the night, they awakened to find glowing eyes and a cloud of white hair floating over their bed. La Chatte shook Crellon's shoulder and then Jacques'.

"Come and see, come and see," the old woman chanted. "The King of France is in misery."

The dim glow of embers in the fireplace let them see Madame Fredôme hanging over them. Jacques, the weaver's son, whispered in panic, "She's here, right beside me."

Crellon, now fully awake, cautioned his friend. "Remember, do not cry out. My Uncle Chandoore does not know about La Chatte. He would have her beaten if he knew."

Jacques shuddered, then after a long moment, he whispered, "I am no longer afraid. See? She beckons to us."

"Are you willing to follow?" asked Crellon.

La Chatte's entreaty became more urgent. "Come and see the King of France's misery. But have a care, have a care! Too many guards are on the stair." She glided first to the bedchanber door, opened it ever so carefully to peep out into the gallery, then closed the door noiselessly.

Crellon was at her elbow. He asked, "How can we get by the guards without rousing them?"

Madame crossed the chamber to the opposite wall. She laid her hand on one of the polished wood panels. "I know a way between wall and wall." The panel slid behind the one next to it. "Don't trip, young sires, lest you fall."

Thoughts raced through Crellon's head, crowding one against another for consideration. "I will follow you, Madame. But Jacques, perhaps you had better stay here. My uncle would not hesitate to kill us if we are caught."

But Jacques insisted on going through the opening with Crellon.

From a recess in the blocks of stone, Madame Fredôme took a lantern with a single candle in it. She glided to the fireplace and from its coals obtained a light for the candle. Then, satisfied, she returned to the other side of the doorway and returned the panel to its place in the wall. She beckoned to the boys. "Softly, softly, that's the way. We've closed the panel without delay."

In the meager light of the candle, Crellon and Jacques could see the scaffolding that tied wooden interior structure to the outer stone wall of the castle. "Watch your footing, down past the rafter; one slip now, you'll regret it after."

Down they climbed, all three, past the rough masonry of the great hall's fireplace. Sometimes with barely a handhold until the next foot touched a firm support, sometimes inching along a ledge, coming to close-crowded beams through which they had to squeeze. But always La Chatte was one step ahead of the boys, knowing exactly the safe route, knowing exactly where she was leading them.

Her hand went up to warn them to be still. "Listen, young sires, and you can learn best what le Compte Chandoore says to his unwilling guest."

Crellon, realizing that they had descended perhaps a hundred feet between the walls, blurted out in astonishment, "Why, we must be close to the dungeon keep!"

"Hist!" warned La Chatte, for now they could hear, faintly, voices and the rattle of chains over the drip, drip of water.

Jacques was first to recognize the King's voice. "Why don't you kill me and have done with this business?" they heard the King demand. "You have kept me in chains for months. I would rather die than delay the Crusade."

"It is the King!" whispered Crellon. "At latest report, he was expected in Nice weeks ago. Why is he here?" And the Duc's son learned why when the next voice was heard.

"That, among other things, I have accomplished," boasted Le Compte Chandoore. "I have, of a certainty, delayed the Crusade."

"Traitor!" screamed the King of France.

"Shriek if you must till you lose your voice," hissed Chandoore. His oily tones were a torment to the King. "No one will hear you. You are worth nothing to me dead. One of the Saracen leaders is bargaining for the privilege of personally parting you from your head."

"How long have you planned this treachery?" demanded His Majesty.

Chandoore, enjoying the King's anger and his discomfort, took pleasure in explaining. "I plan nothing. I let each action fall into place, and play my part as the opportunity presents itself. Once my brother placed his keys in my hands, and you determined to set off early and alone, it was easy to lead you here in search of stronger armor. And are you not now the best-guarded secret in the castle? But once I had you here, little bird in your cage, I began to wonder how this situation could be useful to me. Then, and only then, did I see my chance of doing business with my Turkish friends."

The King raged at the mocking insolence of Chandoore. "I don't know who is the bigger cutthroat, you or Saladin!"

Through the silky smoothness of Chandoore's speech rock-hard determination could be heard. "You may argue that point for the balance of the night, mighty Majesty, but you will eat. I am determined that Philip Augustus must be alive when I deliver him into the hands of the Seljuk merchants. Now, eat."

La Chatte held the boys in steady silence until they heard a clanging of the iron gate to His Majesty's cell. Then she pulled them along until they came to a narrow slit in foundation walls. Through this Crellon and Jacques crawled to find themselves in the dungeon guardroom, outside an iron-barred alcove in which the King of France was chained to the wall. La Chatte waved the boys closer to the King, cautioning them to maintain quiet.

"Your Majesty," whispered Crellon, "I am Crellon, son of Duc de Bresserie. And you will remember my friend Jacques. We have come to free you."

The King looked first to the young men, then to Madame Fredôme. "Have a care," he cautioned. "The guards are ever watchful. I am afraid there is nothing two young lads can do to help me."

"But there is," said Jacques. "We can find Crellon's father, and mine, and bring them back to liberate you."

The King considered what had been said by his two loyal subjects. He weighed the possibilities of their suggestion. "Then there must be no alarm, or Le Compte Chandoore's men will quickly put you and me out of the way. All must be accomplished stealthily and with no advance warning."

There were sounds in the distant vaults of the dungeon; Crellon stole a glance over his shoulder. "La Chatte can show us how to slip past the guards. We can borrow horses from the villagers and be in Nice in four days' time."

The King shook his head sadly. "You will have to be swifter than that. Your uncle will sell me to Saladin's spies within the week."

Jacques had a counter-proposal. "Should we go to neighboring knights for help? The Baron Freis is one day's ride away."

The King turned up his hands in despair. "I cannot advise you. Baron Freis has refused before to help me. Counsel with Duchesse de Bresserie. Explain to her what you have discovered and she will know what to do."

La Chatte, who had been peering through the iron lattice of

the guardroom door, now tugged at Crellon's sleeve. "Withdraw now, young sires," she begged. "The night grows short and the sleeping guard stirs."

"Go carefully," cautioned the King. "Do not betray Madame Fredôme. She has been my one consolation these many days."

At the sound of the patrol's boots on the stone floor, La Chatte scooped up her lantern and beckoned the boys toward their escape. Without a word and with hardly a sound they climbed between the walls, up and up, until they set foot once more in Crellon's bedroom.

In the shadowy light of dawn, Madame Fredôme led Crellon and Jacques to a high mirror, which swung back at her touch. It opened onto another secret passage, leading round several cubicles to the castle's master chamber. Madame touched a lever, a door snapped open, and Crellon stood beside his mother's bed. In the urgent desire to avoid startling the Duchesse, he touched his fingers to her lips. "Quietly, mother. You must not cry out. It is La Chatte and Jacques and me. We have discovered Uncle Chandoore's treachery."

The Duchesse sat up among her pillows. "Whatever are you talking about, Crellon? And how did you get here?" She reached for her dressing gown. "I keep the door to my bedchamber bolted."

"We came by a secret passage," Crellon explained. "We are sorry for frightening you but our chief concern is that my uncle keeps the King of France a prisoner in the castle dungeon."

The Duchesse rose from her bed, but La Chatte signalled for her to avoid making any noise. Ever so quietly, she stole to the bedchamber door, slid the bolt and looked cautiously into the corridor beyond. Satisfied, she closed the door and shot the bolt. Now she nodded knowingly.

"The King?" asked the Duchesse. "Still in Chateau Bresserie? How can that be? He was away before dawn on the day Duc Roland set out for the Holy Land."

"So Uncle Chandoore told us. But Mother, the King languishes in chains and he begs you to tell us how best we can rescue him."

"The King in chains, and my Roland far away!" wept the Duchesse. "We are but women and children. How can we possibly outwit a scheming, treacherous knight?"

"It could be, my lady," Jacques ventured timidly, "that we could ride to bring help from neighboring knights."

The Duchesse de Bresserie assessed this suggestion. "If there are knights at home in neighboring lands, they are either too old to care what happens to the King, or they have refused the King's invitation to join him in the Crusade. We could count on neither to come to the King's rescue." She took a few steps towards the window.

La Chatte followed her. "I must tell you, my Mesaline," she said in a voice strangely like the Duc's, "that your distrust of le Compte Chandoore is doubly justified. He has dealings with the Saracens. I have heard him, in the dead of night, striking bargains with mysterious visitors to surrender the King" and here her tone changed so that, uncannily, she repeated the words of Chandoore—"for three thousand pieces of gold and title to Chateau Bresserie!"

Suddenly, it all came clear to the Duchesse. Her world had been caught up, enmeshed in a vast pattern of treason and bribes, treachery and ransom, political trickery and barbarous double-dealings. To escape was one small consideration; to rescue the King, another. To shake out the wrinkles of plots and counterplots, to thwart the ambitions of wicked men and further the causes of those who strove for honesty and sincerity—these were the forces that could right her world again. She saw that the aims established by the King for his Crusade were even more a necessity here in France.

And now she saw what must be done. Calmly, she set out the facts so that her young knights might understand. "Clearly, we need help. We need to be rescued from Chandoore's grip. It would mean death for all of us if the castle were stormed. Whatever is done to undo your uncle's system of snares and traps must be brought about just as secretly, as insidiously as he has proceeded in setting up the snares and traps. We have only one course of action and, Crellon and Jacques, it falls on your shoulders to carry it out. Ride far beyond the castle wall, to Rheims, and Dijon, and Nice, and bring back the Lord of Chateau Bresserie."

La Chatte bobbed up and down in agreement. "Chandoore must be caught off guard by the return of the Duc. I shall take Crellon's place in the household, wearing his clothes, doing what he usually does, being careful at all times not to meet up with Le Compte Chandoore. If you approve, Duchesse, I will help your faithful knights to cross the moat before broad daylight."

Jacques wanted to put the Duchesse's mind at ease. He said, "We will be cautious, my lady."

Crellon said bravely, "No need, we can swim the moat, Madame Fredôme."

La Chatte cackled at the idea. "And ride all day in wet clothing?" she scoffed. Then, more kindly, she explained. "No, Crellon, we will cling to the drawbridge and ride down on it when it is lowered for the baker with today's bread."

"That is clever strategy," said Crellon. "I hope my clothing fits you well. Wear my cap and pull it down the way I do, and none of Chandoore's cutthroats will know you are not son of the Duc de Bresserie."

The Duchesse placed her hands on the shoulders of her son and his friend. "Go safely, young knights. I cannot trust you to better hands than those of La Chatte."

In the bright, cool light of early morning, three figures picked their way carefully to the top of the portcullis. When the cry came for the drawbridge to be lowered, as La Chatte had predicted, two of the three took handholds on the bridge beams and swung out, dangling from the timbers, and not even the sleepy baker noticed them. As the bread cart rumbled over the bridge, Crellon and Jacques cut across the green meadow as quickly as they could. They hurried through the woods to the village, where they found themselves among willing, helpful friends.

With borrowed horses, the sons of Duc and weaver rode off, beyond the castle lands, in service of the King of France.

Meanwhile, during the week that followed, the Duchessse and her daughters, with Madame Fredôme disguised as Crellon, carried out their daily programs, giving no suspicion that Le Compte Chandoore's treason was known to them.

Whenever any of the spying henchmen hired by Chandoore came within hearing, they played their roles well.

"Come, Crellon," Valerie would sing out. "Climb the tree and make a swing for us."

"No, no!" Madeleine would cry in contradiction. "Come to the fields for a picnic. Bordolaire will pack us a basket!"

They dared not explain to Bordolaire why Madame Fredôme was masquerading as Crellon, nor did they need to. The faithful cook was a loyal friend, and did all the small things she could to give them comfort and courage during each passing day.

But at night, the little family huddled together in fear and trembling. "And have any of you seen Le Compte Chandoore this afternoon?" asked the Duchesse. "I try to keep aware of his movements."

"Yes, we saw him," replied Madeleine. "He was standing on the parapet watching us until we waved and blew kisses to him. Then you could see him scowl, even at that distance, and he turned away. He must hate us with all his heart, Mama."

The Duchesse sighed. "You must not let Chandoore's hatred hurt you, dear daughter. It is good for us that he plays out his part openly; in this way we are warned to be ever on guard. Let me see: this is the seventh day—have Crellon and Jacques been gone only a week?"

"But Mama," protested Madeleine, "they are only boys. They cannot ride over a hundred miles a day."

Little Valerie, feeling the tension and pressure of their confined existence, cried "They must! they must!" in hysteria.

"Oh, I wish I didn't know! I can't keep pretending I don't know!"

There was the hushed sound of a panel sliding, and La Chatte stood in their midst. "You must; you will," she said. "I have just come from the King. He has given up hope because I told him what I heard on my way down to the dungeon. Chandoore expects to surrender the King's person to the Seljuks tonight at midnight. I shall ride down on the drawbridge and try to frighten away the Turks."

The Duchesse considered La Chatte's suggestion and agreed to employing her strategy. "There's still a chance," she said hopefully. "And if that fails, I can confront Chandoore with his perfidy. If I can catch him off guard, perhaps I can shock him into changing his plan."

"Please, no," begged La Chatte. She pivoted and danced away into the shadows. "You must promise to stay locked in this chamber until I come to let you out." Her voice trailed off into the darkness as she chanted, "It matters not what happens to me, but your son will one day be Duc de Bresserie."

"She's gone, as quietly as she came," breathed Madeleine. "I wish I could follow her."

"We must wait and trust La Chatte," said the Duchesse with determination. "Turn the hourglass, Valerie. We must not lose track of time."

While the Duchesse and her daughters waited suspensefully, le Compte Chandoore sat beside the fireplace in the great hall, also waiting for time to pass.

"Will it never be midnight," mused Chandoore, "so that I can have done with this transaction? I care nothing for the King of France, but both he and I could sleep peacefully the night if it were not for the mysterious customs of the Seljuks."

From the watchtower came a brazen clanging. "Ah, the curfew bell!" he muttered. He hurried to the window that looked out onto the tower. "Soon, soon, the flaming arrow signal must show."

All seemed peaceful as Le Compte peered unblinking into

the midnight darkness. But within minutes, an arrow with a flaming tail arched over the parapets of the castle.

Below, at the portcullis, the drawbridge chains began to creak and Madame Fredôme rode down on the bridge until it settled into its sockets. From the other side of the moat came a whisper.

"Madame Fredôme—over here! I knew it was you clinging to the planks." Madame identified the voice as Jacques Portraine's. "The Duc and Crellon are hidden in the clump of cypress, close at hand."

"Let them be," cautioned La Chatte. "They must see and hear what is about to happen."

Now Chandoore's guardsmen rammed torches into the brackets on both sides of the portcullis. There were muffled footsteps as Chandoore came striding into the center of the drawbridge. "Come out of the shadows, you Saracen dog," commanded Chandoore. "I've had enough of this stealth. I want to deal openly."

A slight, wiry figure in filmy cloak and silken leg-coverings glided onto the drawbridge. "I have your gold ready to put into your hands, mighty Chandoore. Have you the treasure I seek to buy?" The Saracen rubbed his hands together in anticipation.

Chandoore laughed, then purred in his velvet voice, "What kind of fool do you take me for? I will deliver you the King of France when I receive the gold."

The Saracen gave a silent signal and out of the night came two sweating servants, carrying bags heavy with gold coins that chinked as they were dragged to the drawbridge center. Chandoore tore open the ties on one of the sacks and, reaching in, scooped up a handful of the coins. "Ah, three thousand pieces weigh heavily. But you will find the merchandise worth the price." He let the coins drop back into the bag. "Wait patiently and I will deliver to you the King of France." And Chandoore retired into the shadows of the castle wall.

As soon as the villainous half-brother was beyond earshot, the Duc de Bresserie sprang onto the bridge, surprising his adversary. "I have my fingers at your throat, O Saracen. Do I dispatch you at once, or do I bind and gag you against my brother's return?"

The Saracen struggled against Duc Roland's grip, then suddenly admitted, "I am your prisoner, Mighty one. Let no blood be shed."

"You have made a wise decision, and I shall spare your life. Come, Crellon, quickly. Thrust a gag between his teeth while I tie him up. We must make certain he will not interfere with the action to come."

When Crellon and the Duc had trussed up the Seljuk merchant and his helpers, they rolled the helpless conspirators into the shadows alongside of the moat. "Stand guard over these, my son. I have a score to settle with your uncle." The Duc quickly crossed the drawbridge and flattened himself against the castle wall, to one side of the portcullis, waiting for the return of Chandoore.

Below in the dungeon, Chandoore unlocked the King's iron cuffs. "You will come quietly, Philip Augustus," hissed Chandoore, "or my guards will cut you down."

"Why should I follow you when you should be following me?"

"So," sneered Chandoore, "now we come to the crux of it. My mother, the Princess Mirizshah, has trained me to recognize the true infidel. Move, Majesty, or I shall smite you."

Reluctantly, King Philip Augustus left his prison, prodded by Chandoore, who continued his harangue. "The true infidel is not the poor mendicant who comes visiting religious shrines, but is the knight who slays innocent people in the name of faith, hope, and charity, scheming to win by conquest what he has lost centuries ago through indolence, avarice and irreverence."

The King paused on a landing at the head of the dungeon

stairs. The thought struck him that he should argue the point with his adversary, but Chandoore was in no mood for debate. He shoved the King roughly toward the portcullis. "Mind your footing on the drawbridge, Philip Augustus. The Turks did not bargain for a dead king."

"Nor I for a treacherous kinsman!" Duc Roland strode into the center of the portcullis, cutting off Chandoore's retreat. "On guard, Chandoore!" shouted Roland, and the half-brothers drew their swords. Crellon and Jacques crept forward to draw the dazed King to one side, away from the thrust and parry. Crellon watched in fascinated horror as the swords flashed in the torchlight. He noticed for the first time how closely his father and uncle resembled each other: each was the son of the old Duc. Their swords were almost identical, having been selected from their father's armory. Their footwork was evenly matched, instinctively patterned after similar fencing techniques. At last a difference became apparent—determination. "I am coming for you, Chandoore!" shouted the Duc. "Only one of us may stand when this swordplay is over!"

Chandoore threw down his sword, "Enough!" he cried. "Do with me what you will. I will fight no more!"

Roland raised his blade to strike, but the King commanded "Hold, de Bresserie! Do not run him through. Chandoore has taunted me so often in the past months, and but a few moments ago he lectured me on the true crusading spirit. I want an opportunity to speak with him at length on forgiveness and repentance."

"As you wish, my King," conceded the Duc.

"Put him in my cell in the dungeon; shackle him with my cuffs and chains. I shall visit him tomorrow to demonstrate my forgiveness and give him opportunity to repent. Until he does, let him know the agony of hopeless imprisonment."

The Duc recognized that Philip Augustus had become once again the iron-willed King of France.

Madame Fredôme, having witnessed the Duc's victory over Chandoore and the liberation of the King, scampered away to inform the Duchesse and her daughters. The Duc left Crellon, Jacques and the King to guard the prisoners and returned in a short while with loyal guardsmen, who hauled the conspirators off to the dungeon.

Even though it was now well past midnight, the Duc roused members of the household staff and commanded them to establish the King in Chandoore's luxurious quarters. At this point, the Duchesse came hurrying through the great hall to welcome her husband and son home. With her came Madeleine and sleepy Valerie, trailed by a happy Madame Fredôme.

"Dear husband," sang the Duchesse, "your return is double cause for rejoicing, for just in time you have saved the King, and you have rescued us from the tyranny of Chandoore."

"The King is indeed safe," the Duc assured his wife, "while Chandoore languishes in the same chains the King wore. Come, Mesaline, we and the children must get some rest. And you, also, Madame Fredôme. The night grows short."

"But you are home, Papa! Say you are home to stay!" demanded Madeleine.

The Duc smiled down at his daughter as they began mounting the great staircase. But there was regret in his voice when he said, "We will talk about that tomorrow. The King of France will not readily give up his Crusade."

When they reached the bedchambers, Valerie took Madame Fredôme's hand. "Come, spend the night with us," she coaxed, and Madeleine added her voice to the invitation.

Madame Fredôme tilted her head and murmured, "Know you not that I must be about my business? Le Compte Chandoore is now in chains, and I must hear how he complains." She followed Crellon into his bedchamber; the two boys heard the whisper of a sliding panel, and she was gone. "I wish she had let us go with her," said Jacques.

"She may, in time," said Crellon, throwing himself wearily onto his bed.

In the morning, the King paid his promised visit to Chandoore. The wicked knight was unrepentant and defiant. Though the King pleaded with Chandoore to declare his allegiance and follow the call to Crusade, the fallen knight remained adamant and Philip Augustus abandoned hope of making another Christian and winning another crusader.

When he had returned from the dungeon, the King found that the Duc de Bresserie had assembled the household in the great hall.

"Come, breakfast with us, Sire," urged the Duchesse, and when the invitation was accepted, they sat down to eat the finest food Bordolaire could assemble at such short notice.

Hunger satisfied, the King spoke. "We are chiefly grateful to the two young squires, Crellon and Jacques, who so bravely rode out to bring home the Duc. It was a great service they performed for the crown and the Crusade. They have indeed earned their armor. I bid them come forth that I may do them honor."

Crellon and Jacques, startled by the royal command, knelt before the King, who gently laid his sword blade on each young man's shoulder, pronouncing them knights of the realm. To this he added, "I absolve the Duc de Bresserie from further service, since he is needed here. As for me, I must go on. The pilgrimage must still be made, the battle must still be won. Know that France will ever by indebted to Crellon and Jacques, knights of the King's Crusade."

The Tree of Bells

China

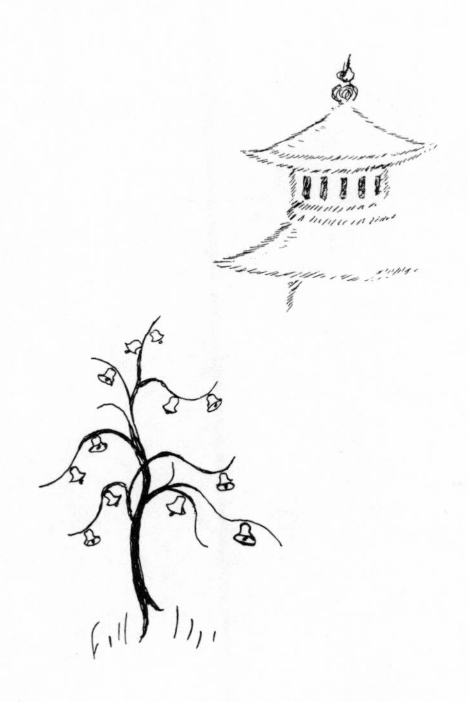

Many long centuries ago, there lived in China a kind and good Emperor whose name was Quo Ming. The great Emperor Quo Ming made it his daily habit to visit the craftsmen of his empire. His eagerness to see and know what each must master to excel in his art was exceeded only by his desire to work side by side with the master craftsmen in the making of an exceptional piece of work in that art form.

One fine morning the Emperor, followed by his Empress, Li Sung, and their son, Prince Quai, appeared in the foundry of the most famous bellmaker in all China. So much smoke rose from the fires that the Empress, her eyes smarting, declared that she could not see. It was indeed dark inside the foundry, which had no windows and only one door.

"Cannot the bellmaker work in the fresh air and sunlight?" asked the Empress. The Emperor explained patiently that the foundry must be so built as to prevent drafts on the boiling metal.

At that moment the bellmaker shouted that the metal was almost ready to pour. "Quickly, my Emperor! If it is your will to help me, pump on the bellows to fan the fire. I need a great draft to make the metal hot enough to flow easily."

The Emperor agreed readily and began to pump with great energy. Prince Quai stood at his father's elbow, watching with great interest. "I cannot understand, my father. You say the foundry is built without openings to prevent drafts. Yet now, the sweat stands on your brow as you stir up a great gale of a draft because the bellman says he needs it."

The Emperor smiled, knowing that many things are beyond the comprehension of a young boy. As he pumped the handle of the bellows rapidly up and down he said, " It may be that you must labor hard to grasp the import of this lesson. Here, take the bellows, my son, and try your hand at fanning the fire."

Prince Quai took the handle and pumped industriously. His mother, the Empress, admired the bright burst of flame. " It is a beautiful fire, stirred by the princely hand of my son. Can it be, dear husband, that the great labor has wearied you?"

The Emperor smiled at his wife's astute observation and was about to reply, but the bellman, bent over his fiery ladle, called out, " Now we are ready, great Emperor Quo Ming. Do not be frightened, Empress, when the molten metal meets the mold. The sand will sputter and scream: this puts voice into the bell. Steady now! Stand back, Prince Quai!"

At the bellman's signal, he and the Emperor grasped the handles of the ladle, carried it, hissing and glowing, to the casting box then tilted the ladle so that its lip met the trough pressed into the sand. Purring like a cat, the liquid metal crept into the hollow mold.

"Ah, this will be the finest bell in all China!" panted the bellmaker. "Never before has an Emperor lent a hand in the casting of a bell. We shall call it the 'Bell of Quo Ming!' "

The Emperor stood back, wiping perspiration from his face and smiling, content with his participation in this creative act. The bellman, noting his Emperor's pleasure, said, "I will deliver the bell to your palace as soon as it has been cooled and tuned."

The Empress drew her husband aside and hissed into his ear. "Quo Ming! What shall we do with a bell in our imperial residence? Do not clutter up the palace with one more sample of your dabbling in the arts and crafts! Last week it was Ming vases; and now—." Vexed, she turned away.

Quo Ming attempted to soothe his wife by promising, "Have no fear, dear Li Sung. The bell shall go to a suitable temple as a gift from the imperial family." When he turned once more to the bellmaker, he said, "I thank you for this delightful lesson. The bell, unfortunately, is too large to install in the imperial palace. But if you will send it, after it has been properly voiced, to the Temple of Angry Wives, I shall be forever grateful." To this pronouncement he managed to add, so softly that Li Sung took no notice, "I would like to come back tomorrow to make some bells—little ones that will not take up too much space at home."

Early next morning, the Emperor began to make his bells: some gold, some silver, a few the size of the Empress's hand, then tinier and tinier until the last was cast in a mold carved from a peach stone.

However charming and dainty these small bells were, they did not for one moment make Li Sung happy. She bore with them patiently until the final bell was presented to her at dinner several days later.

"Forty nine bells, Quo Ming!" the Empress scolded. "There is room on the imperial dinner table for not one more bell!" She picked up two of the larger ones and jangled them under his nose.

The Emperor defended his work. "But they are imperial bells, cast by my own hand," he protested. "That alone makes them unique."

The Empress, losing patience, answered, "So were the pottery jugs, and these very cups, to say nothing of the hundred other objects you have made! You have turned the palace into a museum, filled with things we are afraid to use, and why? Simply because they have been turned, or cast, or carved by your imperial hand."

Prince Quai, whose tutors had drilled him in the strictest forms of court protocol, coughed politely to indicate to his parents that he had something to say. When, as protocol demanded, they turned their attention to him, Prince Quai announced, "Dear parents, I have thought of a way to use these beautiful bells. In the garden, we have a lonely, withered willow tree. It would have grown straight and strong if the soil had not been stony."

"Then," interrupted the Emperor impatiently, "dig out the stones, Quai my son, as your father would."

The Prince hid a smile as he bowed low. "One moment, my father," said Quai. "You placed the stones there, in the imperial rock garden. But it would do no good now to change the soil, the gardener tells me. All I propose is that we hang these bells on the tree, to give it a mark of beauty; a little something that other trees do not have."

The Emperor was pleasantly surprised by his son's suggestion, but the Empress's delight was without bounds. "Oh, excellent, Quai!" she exclaimed. "It will be our own tree of bells. There will be no other like it in all China. And husband, as they swing in the breeze, the bells will be heard, as you have wanted them to be."

And so the Tree of Bells came into being. The little gnarled willow, proudly bearing its gold and silver burden, soon became known far and wide as the loveliest tree in the imperial gardens. The palace servants enjoyed its music as much as did the royal family, and one warm afternoon found Reed Song, a little maid of linens, sitting in the shade of the tree of bells. The tinkling song of the bells seemed an invitation to Reed Song.

"Oh, prettiest of trees," said the little maid, "your cool shadow is almost as sweet as your song. Can you know how happy you make everyone who sees and hears you?"

The tree tinkled a merry laugh. "Yes, Reed Song, a tree knows many things." And when Reed Song started in fright, the tree added, "Please do not run away. You have no cause to be afraid."

Reed Song, stopped in her flight by the plea of the tinkling tree, brushed a hand over her eyes. "I must be sunstruck!" she thought. "The heat is making my ears ring, and I think I hear—."

"You do, little one," murmured the tree. "Now that I have found a voice, I must have someone to hear me. For I am kin to trees in many lands and many places. I know from them what is, and what shall be."

The little maid of linens considered what she had been told. She had been trained from childhood in an understanding that such exalted privileges as speaking with a tree of bells should be reserved for ancestors or royalty. For this reason she said, "You must let me call the Emperor so you may speak with him."

But the tree of bells was not to be persuaded. "No," the tree replied. "The Emperor will not hear what you hear. He cannot understand me as you can." Reed Song bowed in humility, and in a moment she heard the tree continue. "Still, I will be useful to the Emperor and Empress, one day, and to Prince Quai, who first thought of the Tree of Bells."

Reed Song was amazed by the extent of the tree's knowledge of what had happened and of what people had thought, and she could not believe that she had been chosen, above others, to receive the tree's message. She protested, "What can I, a poor maid of linens, do with my ability to speak with you? Will anyone believe me? Will anyone trust that I speak truthfully?"

The Tree of Bells seemed to grow impatient at this stream of questions. She tossed her branches; her musical reply was "Wait and see, Reed Song. First go to Quo Ming, mighty Emperor of China, and tell him that the royal merchant barques are on their homeward journey, and that all goes well with them. They will cross the Bay of Japan in three days, and on the morning of the fourth, they will be sighted in the great harbor."

Now, Prince Quai had been working in the garden that hot summer day. When he heard Reed Song's voice, he stepped behind a clump of lilacs to listen. At this moment he could not suppress his curiosity any longer. "What are you doing here, little maid?" he demanded. "Why are you not doing your chores?"

Reed Song dropped to her knees and bowed low. "I have

done all my chores, Prince Quai, and I stopped but a moment in the cool shade. If you will permit me, I will go."

Prince Quai, regretting the scolding tones in which he had spoken, pleaded, "Please forgive my making you uncomfortable. I could not help hearing you speak to the Tree of Bells."

Reed Song, looking up, explained, "It is not of my choosing. The tree insisted that I must go tell your father, Emperor of All China, that all is well with his merchant ships. I know it sounds strange to give a message like this."

"Have no fear, little one. My father is kind and good. I will take you to him myself."

Reed Song thought the offer was really kind on the part of Prince Quai, and so she said. But having made the offer, the Prince began to consider cautiously how he should present Reed Song to the Emperor. And, besides, "What proof have we that the tree really spoke to you? Oh, don't think I doubt your word, but my father sits this afternoon with the seers and deputies of the empire, and they and the Emperor will require some sign."

The Tree of Bells jangled a melody which Prince Quai could not understand. "Do not worry, Reed Song," said the tree. "The gentlemen of the household, even the deputies themselves, will make way for you if you whisper the words 'Wings of Thunder'."

Prince Quai was bursting with excitement. "What does the tree say?" he asked. "Can you understand?"

"The tree told me to whisper 'Wings of Thunder.' But if the Emperor will take offense, my Prince—"

"Wings of Thunder!" Quai exclaimed. "That is the secret navy password for this month. Come quickly. My father will certainly listen to what you have to tell him." Thereupon the Prince of China hurried Reed Song through the gardens and across the cool verandahs of the palace and into the imperial reception room where the Emperor sat surrounded by the seers and sages of the Empire.

Quai, as befitted a Chinese prince in the presence of the Emperor and his advisors, awaited a nod of recognition from his father. "My son?" murmured the Emperor kindly.

Quai made an elaborate bow and began. "Imperial father, I come to you unannounced because I have learned something most interesting and of great importance to the Empire."

The deputies voiced their surprise, the seers nodded as they understood the mystery of Quai's announcement, yet the Emperor and his chief soothsayer, the Prime Minister Sin Yang, trained looks of bewilderment on the young Prince.

"What is this puzzle which you pose, Quai?" asked the Emperor. "Is this another of your games?"

Sin Yang, looking like a statue of polished ivory, sneered, "His playmate is naught but a chambermaid. She can provide little of interest to this conclave." He raised a fan to block Reed Song from his sight.

The Emperor considered the wisdom expounded by his prime minister; then, disregarding it, he turned to Reed Song. "And you, little flower, what brings you here?" he asked.

Impatiently, Prince Quai began to explain. "It is not of her choosing, Father."

The Emperor raised an imperial hand. "One moment, young sir. I will hear the girl speak for herself."

Reed Song, gathering her courage and now unafraid, told the Emperor, "The Tree of Bells has spoken to me, O Father of us all. My name is Reed Song, and the tree bids me say that all is well with the royal barques on the rolling seas; that the Emperor's captains bring home cargoes of treasure magnificent and beautiful, sparkling with gems and crusted with gold."

Sin Yang, who enjoyed a reputation as an imperial soothsayer, began to cackle in derision. "Anh! The child speaks foolishness. How could the singing tree tell her all this?" Then, seeing that the Emperor was not properly impressed with his question, Sin Yang continued. "Beware, great

Emperor Quo Ming. She may be the pawn of your enemies, spying for the robber Mandarins!"

The Emperor, noting that he had displeased his old advisor, said apologetically, "Yours are weighty words, Sin Yang, and you have served my Empire for many years, having advised my father before me. Yet, though you are the Imperial Soothsayer, you have voiced no such predictions."

Sin Yang flicked his fan furiously, then snapped it as he exclaimed, "Bah! Anyone can dream up such messages as these!"

Prince Quai began to fear his father would dismiss Reed Song's message as nonsense. "But Father," he argued, "I tell you I saw and heard Reed Song speak."

"Then let me hear Reed Song speak for herself. By what authority do you bring me this tale, little one?"

Reed Song stared at the Emperor's sandals and said in awe, "By the 'Wings of Thunder', my Emperor."

From beside the Emperor's left elbow, a short, fat deputy spoke up. "The child knows of what she speaks," he said. "She speaks in the words of the month."

Sin Yang, agitated, rose from his seat and paced the length of the conference room. "She has bewitched Prince Quai," he sputtered. "She has wormed the secret words from him by trickery!"

"That cannot be, Sin Yang," replied the Emperor. "My son is under no spell. His eyes are not befogged by witchery."

Another sage who sat at the far end of the conference table spoke. His flashing green eyes, like glittering emeralds, emphasized his pronouncement. "The gods have sent you a seeress, great Majesty. They know that old Sin Yang cannot live much longer."

Sin Yang drew a slender dagger from the handle of his fan and with one swift motion pinned the long, silken sleeve of the green-eyed sage to the conference table. "I have learned the secret of eternal life, you fool!" he spat. "Was I not this old when you were a boy in the great Ming navy? But this little witch will wither and die before you draw your last breath, though you be ninety-three on your next birthday!"

Not at all dismayed by Sin Yang's display of violence, the aged green-eyed sage addressed the Emperor of China. "Great Quo Ming, it is true that I served in your grandfather's navy in my youth, and I am now old. But I can see that one innocent message makes this girl neither seeress nor witch. If Sin Yang wishes to prove his usefulness to the empire, let him, too, learn the language of the Tree of Bells."

As Sin Yang retrieved his dagger, the Emperor said, "Do not let this quarrel frighten you, Reed Song. Go, play, my child, and if the Tree of Bells speaks to you again, bring me its message." He patted Reed Song's hand.

"I must only say that four days from now the ships will come into harbor."

The little maid of linens shuddered as Sin Yang bellowed. "Now we will catch her in her lies!" In fury, the soothsayer threw a handful of powder into a nearby incense urn; angry flames and smoke poured into the conference room. In the confusion that followed, Prince Quai led Reed Song away from the council chamber.

"Come, have tea with me in the garden," suggested Quai.

"Oh, no! I must attend the Mistress of Linens," Reed Song protested. "She will scold me for being away from the linen closet so long."

"Then I will go with you to explain to her," offered Prince Quai. He took her hand, ready to accompany Reed Song.

"Please, you must not. That would frighten the Mistress of Linens and she would scold all the more!" And with that, Reed Song hurried across the verandah and into the dark corridor leading to the domain of the formidable Mistress of the Linens.

The Emperor's merchant ships arrived four days later, as the Tree of Bells had predicted, and there was great rejoicing in the imperial household.

Ko Chan, mighty explorer and leader of the expedition,

paraded through the streets of the city, followed by his splendidly attired company of adventurers and a hundred bearers carrying lavish gifts from beyond the sea.

In audience with the Emperor, Ko Chan held Quo Ming spellbound with his account of adventures in far-away places. "Malaya is the color of cinnamon," Ko Chan declared. "Even its pearls are red and brown together—a great novelty. But Koryo is a bubble of spendor and Kaesong, a city built upon cities, beautiful beyond words, great Quo Ming."

The Emperor murmured "Ah," as was expected of him, and Ko Chan strode about the audience chamber, smiling and smacking his lips in great satisfaction. Suddenly the explorer halted his pacing, poised like a dancer. He clapped his hands and the great jade doors opened to admit a procession of gift bearers and a curtained sedan chair borne by six slaves.

"I have brought treasures of immense value, gold and jewels, spices and rare woods, all for the pleasure of the Emperor of China. But I have brought home a treasure reserved for myself: Koryo's brightest jewel, the Princess Glee Mung, as my bride."

Again the Emperor murmured "Ah," and Ko Chan waved his hand; the slaves gently lowered the sedan to the floor; the bright orange curtains parted and the lovely topaz Princess, Glee Mung, rose to stand before the Emperor of China.

From the sages and dignitaries assembled for the ceremonial return of the explorer came a chorus of "Ahs." Ko Chan bowed and asked the Emperor, "May Glee Mung dance for you?"

The Emperor's eyes devoured eagerly the beauty of the creature who stood before him. Translucent flesh shimmered between the woven silk panels and coin-covered soft leather strips that made up her scant dress. Her hair, each curl wrapped in gold foil, was molded into a large golden tear drop, framing her face and topping a filmy silk veil that covered the lower portion of her face.

Glee Mung bowed, draping her body into a spiral sculpture. "I am—Princess of Kaesong," her velvet voice informed Quo

Ming. "I know very little—how you speak. Ko Chan's bride I be—I dance—yes?"

Quo Ming nodded and Glee Mung danced. A glittering, scintillating series of shoulder and hip motions above precise foot placements that, with the undulations of her arms, gave her performance the sparkle of a magnificent gem. Glee Mung danced, and the members of the Emperor's court fell under her spell. The pace of the Princess of Kaesong's dance increased, with rapid leaps flashing up, then descending in sparrow-like swoopings, low over the floor of the audience chamber. Now everyone joined the Emperor in stamping his foot to beat out the rhythm of Glee Mung's twistings and twirlings. She came to rest at Ko Chan's side.

Quo Ming was greatly pleased by what he had seen, and he thanked the explorer for this delightful surprise. "But you must know, Ko Chan, that I knew you were returning—that I received word of it four days ago."

Ko Chan laughed when he heard the Emperor say this. "Impossible!" he replied. "I did not know myself as early as that. A fresh wind came up and I could not resist running with the breeze."

"Ah, but now we have a way of knowing about such things, apparently before they occur. Come, into the garden. I have a great wonder to show you."

Quo Ming led Ko Chan the explorer and the explorer's bride, the Princess of Kaesong, followed by the Emperor's Prime Minister, Sin Yang, through the open portal into the imperial garden. A lovely, tinkling melody caressed their ears as they approached the Tree of Bells. As the Emperor bowed before the little willow, she chimed in gracious acknowledgment.

"And this is your great wonder?" asked the explorer.

"Indeed it is," replied the Emperor.

Glee Mung went to the tree, touching the branches and bells, and at last the tree's twisted and gnarled trunk. "Tree—very pretty," Glee Mung murmured, and again she fondled several of the bells. She turned to the Emperor, tilted her golden head to one side and said, "You give Glee Mung present for dancing?"

Quo Ming, charmed by her open and seemingly innocent question, assured her. "You shall have a gift from the imperial treasurehouse."

Glee Mung pouted at this reply, then asked, "You give bells to Princess of Kaesong?"

Now the Emperor understood the request and hastened to explain. "We discovered that the Tree of Bells can communicate with us purely by chance. We do not know how the tree acquired the ability to speak, or why it chooses to tell us what is happening elsewhere. If we take away its bells, we take away its voice."

A silent storm distorted Glee Mung's face and she turned away, sparking with spite and wrath. Ko Chan tried to gloss over his bride's tantrum. "I hear the tree sing," he said to the Emperor, "but that is none of the seven languages I know. What does the tree say, Quo Ming?"

The Tree of Bells altered her tune, jangling angrily as if to reflect and respond to Glee Mung's temper. The Princess of Kaesong stood sullenly behind the explorer as the Emperor replied, "It is beyond my understanding, Ko Chan. Reed Song, a household serving maid, can understand and converse with the tree. Then she brings me its message. It is unfortunate that her chores keep her busy today, because she would gladly translate for you the words of the Tree of Bells."

Thereupon, the Emperor led his guests back to the audience chamber while the tree shuddered in fury, causing the bells to clang in discord.

Ko Chan clapped his hands together. Glee Mung bowed low and returned to her sedan. The bright curtains snapped shut and, at Ko Chan's signal, the slaves raised the sedan chair to their shoulders and removed it from the imperial audience chamber.

It was indeed unfortunate that Reed Song did not hear the tree's warning (for warning it was). In the dark of night, Sin Yang, the crafty Prime Minister, went to the chamber of the

Princess of Kaesong who, after a moment's hesitation, admitted him. She held a night lantern close to his face, trying to read its expression.

"What want you—old man?" she demanded. Still, she motioned to the Prime Minister that he should sit beside her on the window seat. "Speak quickly. I know not when my lord Ko Chan returns."

"Have no fear," said Sin Yang. "Your lord and my Emperor have their heads together, planning the next expedition." He laughed, a snickering chortle. "The Empress is furious because they have closed the door to the imperial Chamber of Strategy and locked her out."

"And it is evident—that they—lock you out, also," Glee Mung's grin was luminous by the light of the night lantern.

"Yes. But you have shown, a few hours ago, that you are unhappy, Glee Mung. The Princess of Kaesong should not be unhappy."

Glee Mung shrugged her shoulders, scorning Sin Yang's fawning attempt to win her favor. "Glee Mung pretend," she purred, "but she not unhappy. She know what she know—." The Prime Minister reached out to touch her, but she spun away from him.

"You asked the Emperor for the gold and silver bells. He should not deny you, since you are the bride of the great hero, Ko Chan." Pouting, the golden princess listened to the scheming old man. "But the bells will be yours, if you will do my bidding."

Glee Mung came to kneel beside Sin Yang. "For such payment my services . . . are dependable."

"Then," said the crafty one, "make Ko Chan think it is his own idea, yet send him to the Emperor to suggest taking Prince Quai to sea on his next voyage. That is all I ask of you, and the bells are yours." Now it was Sin Yang's grin that shone in the dim lantern light.

They struck the palms of their right hands together to seal the agreement. Sin Yang glided silently from the Princess's chamber and in the dead of night he stripped the Tree of Bells.

When Quo Ming and Ko Chan wearied of their planning for the next expedition, they unlocked the door of the Chamber of Strategy and went their separate ways, the Emperor stealing silently into the royal bedchamber, careful not to waken Li Sung, his Empress; and the explorer to his assigned apartments where he was greeted by his purring Princess of Kaesong.

It must be said that Glee Mung was the most tantalizing and persuasive of women, the clever mistress of the art of leading her husband to believe that what she suggested was really the product of his own thinking. So carefully was the seed sown, so artfully was it nurtured and cultivated, that by dawn Ko Chan arose, determined to act upon his clever scheme without delay. He woke his golden princess and urged her to pack their chests, to have them ready when he returned from audience with the Emperor.

The Emperor, awakened from pleasant dreams of discovering new ways of using his favorite gemstone, jade, was annoyed by Ko Chan's hurried appearance in the royal bedchamber. Still, he listened to what the explorer had to say.

"I am restless, Quo Ming, and long to be once more at sea. You must know, Quo Ming, that the voyage we have planned will be great and glorious. That is why I would take Prince Quai with me, so that he may learn about the sea—but more—that he may experience the great adventure envisioned by his imperial father. I will guard him and guide him well, and bring him back a wise and wealthy sailor."

The Emperor, on thinking about it, was pleased by the addition of his son to the proposed expeditionary force. Yet, his reply was cautious. "Yours is an excellent plan, Ko Chan, but sudden. It will take some days to win the Empress's consent."

"Surely she will not stand in the way of her son's education. Prince Quai must learn the order of life at sea if he is to be an all-knowing admiral, and a captain of international trade." To this the Emperor listened eagerly. The explorer's reasoning was certainly sound.

"He has never been beyond the reach of Li Sung's voice," said the Emperor, doubt dampening his enthusiasm.

Ko Chan's eyes glittered with anger. "I see I shall have to sail without Quai. But know you that it is an opportunity lost. And in years to come he will not thank you for that loss. I can not possibly return before three years have passed: three years that could shape Quai into a fine young man of the sea." He strode to the windows and opened them wide, surveying the distant harbor.

"But you are in such haste, Explorer!"

Without turning, Ko Chan asked, "Would you have me happy in home port—your most adventurous explorer, unwilling to sail away?"

Quo Ming, Emperor of China, sighed heavily. "No, no," he said. "I will bid the Empress to make her son ready to go to sea." He knew Li Sung would storm long after Ko Chan's sails had dropped below the horizon. "You are right, Explorer. I have kept my son at home too long." He raised his hands and clapped them twice. After a long moment, he clapped them again, asking angrily, "Is there no one in attendance?"

From the folds of the wall hangings a figure stepped into the light of dawn. It was the Prime Minister, Sin Yang. "Is there a service I can perform for my Emperor?"

The Emperor was pleased to have assistance offered so readily. He was tempted to send Sin Yang to break the news to Empress Li Sung. But no, he thought, this is my own particular task. Instead, he told the Prime Minister, "Go rouse the household, Sin Yang. Then wake Prince Quai and tell him that he goes to sea with the great explorer this morning. It will be your special task to help him pack his chests."

Sin Yang bowed low and murmured, "I will be glad to serve the young Prince."

Ko Chan turned from the window. "I must go now to the harbor, Quo Ming. The tide rushes in and we must weigh anchor before midday. I must have everything in readiness for sailing." With four great strides he reached the entrance to the bedchamber, and was gone. In the early light of morning, his image seemed to linger. But no, that was Sin Yang still hovering about the bedpost.

The Emperor dragged himself wearily from his bed. "I must persuade the Empress that this is Prince Quai's golden opportunity." He knocked timidly on the door to his dear Li Sung's chamber and went in, prepared to meet whatever argument she might give with the reasoning that their son must be allowed to grow in wisdom and knowledge through experience in the world outside the imperial palace.

Sin Yang stood at the foot of the Emperor's bed and chortled. "Both are gone about their chores, leaving me to do mine. I shall have the pleasure of packing Prince Quai's chests. And there will be a special little chest, with all the bells from the tree at the bottom—a chest I shall deliver to the Princess Glee Mung, as I promised. Ah yes, she has done her work well, and will be rewarded."

Once Sin Yang had roused the household, a frenzy of preparation whirled young Prince Quai toward the waiting ships, much to his joy. The Empress, as expected, stormed for a while, then capitulated to the Emperor's reasoning. In a few short hours, the imperial family was gathered on the sea wall to the harbor. Even the Emperor had grown somber, knowing that soon he would give his son into the hands of the explorer.

But for Prince Quai it was one of the great exciting events of his life. "Father, I cannot thank you enough for persuading our famous explorer to take me to sea with him! At last I shall be a sailor, and I will make you proud of me—you, and Mother, both. What treasure can I bring you from beyond the seas?"

The Emperor's eyes glittered greedily at the thought of a gift and said, "A yellow diamond, and some oil of musk." These requests were duly noted as the young Prince turned to his mother.

Tears came to the eyes of the Empress. She put her hands on Quai's shoulders. "Bring me nothing but yourself, my son. I knew I would have to let you go adventuring one day. Still, I never dreamt it would be so soon."

"Don't weep, Mother. Ko Chan will guide me and teach me, and in three years, I will return a man."

"Go, then," said the Empress. "The barge is waiting to take you to your ship."

Sin Yang had already heaped the chests into the barge. Prince Quai climbed over them to a seat in the stern, and the bargemen dipped their oars to send the barge skimming over the water to Ko Chan's ship.

The explorer gave his prince a royal welcome; he took Quai into the chartroom to introduce him to the instruments of navigation. Meanwhile, Sin Yang stowed Prince Quai's chests in the assigned quarters, all except the special little chest which he offered to the Princess of Kaesong.

Glee Mung lifted the lid and ran her fingers over the assorted bells. "I may not play with my bells within reach of my husband's ears, for some time to come. Mark the chest well, old man, and store it deep in the hold."

"You have earned your reward," said the old Prime Minister, "and I shall do as you wish." He carried the chest of bells deep into the bowels of the ship, then hurried up to bid farewell to the explorer and Prince Quai. Sin Yang tumbled into the barge as Ko Chan called for lifting of anchors and setting of sails, and the navy of China moved out to sea.

The Empress, Li Sung, found it hard to set an example for other mothers sending their sons to sea for the first time. She would not allow a tear to fall or permit herself a longing glance at the departing vessels. Instead, she spoke a touching prayer for the safe return of the naval expedition—a prayer copied down by the court scribes to be recopied and sent to the people of major cities throughout China.

Similarly, the Emperor busied himself with affairs of state to help pass the first empty day without their son.

Caught up in the excitement of Prince Quai's departure, Reed Song was kept busy in the linen closets until late in the day. But at evening, she stepped into the garden to listen to the music of the tree.

"Not a breath of air stirring," she sighed. "Not a sound from the bells. Perhaps the tree is saddened by Prince Quai's going away." But now she felt a breeze on her cheek, and still there was not music from the bells. Reed Song came close to the little misshapen tree and saw in the twilight that every bell was gone. "What can have happened?" she gasped. "Surely the Emperor has not—."

"Has not what?" rasped Sin Yang who had been standing in the shadows, waiting for the first person who would discover the removal of the bells.

Reed Song, recognizing the Prime Minister, felt free to ask, "Surely the Emperor has not taken the bells away?"

Sin Yang laughed harshly.

"Has he?" Reed Song tried once more to learn what had happened to the bells.

Sin Yang snarled at her. "The Emperor has silenced the tree, as I shall silence you, if you annoy him with any more of your rantings." He shook his fist at the little maid of linens. "There will be no more messages for you to interpret from the Tree of Bells!"

Frightened, Reed Song ran from the garden and hid in a grove of bamboo, far from the palace.

The Emperor and Empress had dined in silence, the Empress not wishing to show how much she regretted allowing the explorer to take her young son far away from home, and the Emperor feeling helplessly unable to comfort his lovely wife. At last the tedious evening came to an end and the Emperor suggested a walk in the garden before they retired to the royal bedchambers. Li Sung agreed readily; she summoned bearers of lanterns to accompany them.

A cool, scented night breeze followed the royal procession along the paths until the Emperor and Empress came quite close to their favorite tree.

"How strange!" exclaimed the Empress. "Not a sound from our little tree. I hoped it would have a message for us."

The full moon had just come up above the roof tops of the palace wings, and the Emperor could see the tree's branches against the bright lunar face. He gasped and pointed. The Empress studied the tree's outline to discover what had so startled her husband. Then she saw that there was not one bell hanging from the bare branches of the little willow.

The Emperor exploded in rage. Who could have done this terrible thing? Who would steal the bells he had made? True, he admitted to the Empress, some were of silver and a few of gold—hardly worth enough to pay a self-respecting robber for the trouble of stealing them. Could it be an enemy, suggested the Empress, someone who would want to deprive the royal family of the bells' voice? And if it were an enemy, then who?

A suspicion stole into the Emperor's mind: the explorer. He had joyfully shown the explorer the Tree of Bells,and had exulted in the tree's ability to transmit messages from far away. The Princess of Kaesong, Ko Chan's dancing wife, had asked for the bells as payment for her dance—and had been denied what she asked.

It seemed clear to the Empress that Ko Chan had stolen their tree's bells to satisfy Glee Mung's desire for the dangling baubles. In great agitation Quo Ming and Li Sung returned to the palace. The Emperor sent messages to summon leaders of the court and in a few minutes the leaders of China, including the Prime Minister, Sin Yang, were assembled in the Room for Strategy.

"I little dreamed, when I showed the tree to Ko Chan, that he in treachery would steal the bells," stormed Quo Ming.

"That may well be why he was in such a hurry to depart," observed the wise man with emerald eyes. "But there may be a more sinister motive," he added. "Is not Prince Quai at this moment in his power?"

Sin Yang snorted, disdainful of the suggestion.

The Emperor saw immediately the true horror of the picture. "Ransom!" he sputtered. "He will hold the imperial heir for ransom! And I alone am to blame, I fell readily into Ko Chan's scheme, disregarding the Empress's protests."

Sin Yang carefully avoided gloating over the Emperor's chagrin. Instead, he stoutly declared his faith in the explorer's good character and intentions. "There is no betrayal in Ko Chan's character. He will care for Prince Quai as earnestly as he serves the Empire."

But the Emperor could not be consoled. He alternately stormed and wept, envisioning his son chained to the planking in the ship's hold.

All this time the Empress had been thinking. It was common knowledge that China had two navies—the imperial navy, captained by rich and famous seamen, like the explorer, Ko Chan; and the navy of pirates and merchants that plied the ports, wresting a living from commerce, local and international. With ease, a group of vessels could be commissioned to follow Ko Chan's fleet, and with favorable winds he would be overtaken by lighter barques skimming before the breeze.

As she pondered these facts, Empress Li Sung began to speculate aloud how Ko Chan might be pursued and Prince Quai be brought home. The Emperor's Council had fallen silent, listening to their Empress's musings.

"A light-hearted pirate could accomplish the mission with ease, and with insult to no one," said the green-eyed sage. "I am in full agreement with Her Imperial Highness. We know only that Prince Quai is at sea with Ko Chan. If we assume more than that, we deceive ourselves and may come to wrong conclusions."

The Emperor agreed with the wise man's logic and urged him to continue. Sin Yang smirked in silence, letting the discussion wander where it might.

"I know of such a pirate," continued the man with green eyes. "A brave fellow who lives by his own code—one who prudently assesses a situation, then dashes fearlessly in to do what must be done. I shall be glad to go to the harbor and seek him out."

"An excellent proposal!" exclaimed the Emperor. "Bring the pirate here so we may commission him to rescue Prince Quai."

There were murmurs of approval among the councilors, but Sin Yang hissed them into silence. "That would be a disastrous tactic," he said. "We cannot afford to let the populace suspect that our imperial heir is in danger. Name the man, and I will go to the waterfront and negotiate for his services, attracting as little public attention as possible."

Sin Yang stood glowering over the green-eyed councilor who reluctantly conceded to Sin Yang's demand. "Chi Pan Ho is the cleverest and most resourceful of China's independent seamen. You will find him under the sign of the Puffing Dragon on the Pier of the Wandering Wayfarers. But you must assure him that he will sail under imperial commands, and that he is fully commissioned to receive the royal person of Prince Quai."

"It shall be done as you say," snarled Sin Yang. But he was greatly pleased. By this strategy, he as Prime Minister had taken control of the council's action and therefore had regained command of the situation. He withdrew as the council continued to deliberate.

Finding Chi Pan Ho was no difficult task for the wily Prime Minister. The waterfront piers crawled with lines of workers loading and unloading vessels and each time he inquired the whereabouts of Chi Pan Ho, he was waved forward along the dock to the last pier, then along that pier until he came to a green barque. Sin Yang leaned over the rail and called, "Chi Pan Ho! Chi Pan Ho! I have a message of great import for you."

From below the deck came a rumbling voice. "Come into the hold, Old Goat, if you want to talk with me."

Sin Yang found a gate in the rail, then crossed the deck to a dark companionway down which he tumbled. "It is a frightful thing for an old man to have to scramble in the darkness."

"Here is a light, you slithering frog. Wait; I'll give you a hand."

Slowly, the eyes of the Prime Minister grew accustomed to the dimness, and he could see the outline of Chi Pan Ho's hulking frame bent over a chart table. Having recovered his footing, Sin Yang stood straight, to his full height, towering over the pirate. "I see you are drawing a map. Can it be a treasure map? A map to pirates' hidden gold?"

Chi Pan Ho turned slowly from his charts. "The curious cat," he thundered, "loses the ninth of his lives if he does not hide his curiosity." Then because it pleased him to do so, he explained. "This map, since you have seen it, marks the path of the warm winds over the Eastern Sea."

"Aha," thought Sin Yang, "I have won the pirate's confidence." So he said, "It is a worthy map for so worthy a captain."

Chi Pan Ho got to his feet, his head among the rafters holding the deck above. He looked down upon Sin Yang. "If you put rings around the words you speak, I'll drown you from the bow. Now speak up; what business have you with me?"

Sin Yang tilted back his head to speak to Chi Pan Ho. "I am the Prime Minister of China."

"Of course you are the Prime Minister. Again I ask: What business have you with me?"

Sin Yang's haughty reply was "I have come to do you a great favor."

"I ask no favors," rumbled Chi Pan Ho. "I work. If you bring me work, I will listen to you. But if you are playing cat and mouse—" He pinched out one of the candles on the chart table.

"Believe what you will," blurted Sin Yang. "I am here to tell you that a king's ransom lies in the bottom of Ko Chan's hold. You have heard of the Emperor's Tree of Bells?"

"Aye! Gold and silver the bells are!" The pirate's eyes glittered at the thought of the value of the bells.

"Ko Chan stole them from the Emperor's garden, not two days ago. Worse still, he holds Prince Quai for ransom." Sin Yang waited until he knew Chi Pan Ho fully understood the situation. Then he added in a soft, sly voice, "The bells and half the ransom are both yours if you follow Ko Chan and bring the prince back to me."

Chi Pan Ho raised his hand as if to strike the old man. Then his anger gave way to disgust. "Yours are slimy schemes. I'll find Ko Chan, but I'll not turn his precious cargo over to you. I'll claim the reward myself. And who knows? I may meet a merchant ship, going or coming, laden with enough booty to add a little profit to the venture. But a word of this agreement to anyone—" Again he raised his hand.

Sin Yang skittered away and started up the companionway. "I shall speak of it to no one," he promised as he turned to the towering giant and said, "Speed on your way and send me word as soon as you can."

Chi Pan Ho lifted the Prime Minister over the rail.

"Have a care!" wailed Sin Yang. "My bones are brittle with age!"

In the privacy of the imperial bedchambers, Quo Ming and Li Sung clung to each other, trying to measure the depth of their troubles, searching for the key to unlock their chain of difficulties. The Emperor was disconsolate over the absence of his son and the loss of the bells. "If only we had the bells we would surely learn how fares our son!" But the bells were gone.

"You must begin all over again," urged the Empress. "Go to the bellmaker and cast a new set of bells. It would be well if Reed Song went with you. She will remember how large each one should be."

But when they went searching for Reed Song, she was not in the House of Linens, and the Mistress of Linens could not remember when she had last seen Reed Song.

Quo Ming tore impatiently through one department after another of the imperial household until he found a water carrier who remembered that Reed Song often visited a certain straw hut in the shadow of the walls of the Imperial City.

There they found her, cowering amid piles of blankets woven by her grandfather. At first Reed Song was too terrified to speak, but little by little the Emperor and Empress drew from her a tale filled with fears of displeasing the imperial family and Sin Yang's threats to silence her if she attempted to translate further messages from the Tree of Bells. No, she did not know who had taken the bells, but she knew that the Prime Minister wished them far away.

The Empress lifted the sobbing girl from her hiding place and together they followed the Emperor as he led the way back to the palace.

"Of this we may be certain," said the Emperor, "it serves Sin Yang's purpose to deny us the voice of the Tree of Bells. You, my dear Li Sung, have urged me to cast a new set of bells. Cast them I shall, but I must confess I do not remember how many there were."

"That I can tell you, my husband," said Li Sung with a sharp edge to her voice. "There were forty-nine bells of various sizes, nearly covering our dining table: the last seven made of gold, stepping down in size from a teacup to a thimble." Then the Empress laughed, recalling her chagrin over those forty-nine bells. The Emperor laughed too, thinking that he could, with the help of his Empress, outwit the wily Prime Minister.

Reed Song laughed as well—a nervous, embarrassed little laugh, not understanding the imperial humor when there was so much to be worried about, to be frightened of, and to be avoided if possible.

Off to the bellmaker went Quo Ming, to begin the task, in great secrecy, of duplicating the bells which gave voice to the little willow tree.

Sin Yang, sitting in the splendor of the Prime Minister's palace, thought of his bargain with the pirate, Chi Pan Ho. He raised his goblet, then set it down. "How will the Fates play out this hand?" he mused. "Will pirate and explorer slay each other? Who will win, in mortal combat?" He shoved the goblet away. "Still, I have done the Emperor's bidding. I have sent an emissary to ransom Prince Quai. And will the Princess of Kaesong be happy with her gold and silver bells? What becomes of China if Prince Quai is slain in battle with the pirates? There is no other heir, and only I have found eternal life. Why then—China will be mine! And I will reward whoever returns, be it pirate or explorer, with death in the Emperor's dungeon."

But the Fates were not all with Sin Yang. The Emperor avoided telling anyone about the new set of bells he was busily casting. Day after day, Quo Ming worked with the bellmaker until after dusk. Late one afternoon, the bellmaker declared, "We have only one more to cast, Quo Ming; just one more: the little one, molded in the stone of a peach."

The Emperor patted the bellmaker's shoulder. "I have already carved the mold. I could not sleep last night. Are you too tired to pour it now?"

"We will pour," said the bellmaker.

"Then let us do it quickly."

"No, not quickly, Quo Ming," replied the bellman. "We must do it precisely as we did before, or the bell will not ring true."

"But will it cool quickly enough so we might hear it tonight?"

"Your tree will speak again, Quo Ming, tonight, tonight."

As soon as the tiniest bell had cooled, the Emperor hurried home with the complete set. Stealthily, he and Reed Song found their way to the willow tree and, by moonlight, they hung the bells on its branches. As they worked, the bells jangled and the Emperor asked, "Does the tree speak, Reed Song?"

"No, " replied the little maid of linens. "It moans so sadly. Let us move some of the silver bells; they do not seem to be on the same branches as before."

Eagerly the Emperor followed Reed Song's directions. And again came a jangling. "Can it now speak?" asked China's Emperor.

Reed Song sighed. "Yes, but faintly. Please move that big bell, Sire. There—"

The Emperor shifted the bell and the tree's branches swayed. From them came the sorrowful voice of the Tree of Bells. "Tell the Emperor to beware the treachery of Sin Yang."

Reed Song translated the tree's message for Quo Ming, who flew into a rage on hearing it. "Girl!" he shouted angrily. "I have no time for your foolish spite against the Prime Minister. I must have word of my son's well-being!"

Reed Song cowered, listening, at the foot of the chiming tree. "Reed Song, make the Emperor understand that Sin Yang plotted to spirit Prince Quai away from China, and that even now a pirate band is pitted against the explorer in the hope that one or the other will destroy the Prince. All are pawns in the game Sin Yang plays."

"What are the bells telling you now?" demanded the Emperor.

"You would not believe me, Majesty. The tree still speaks of treachery and tells of a pirate ship coming close to the explorer's. I can almost see what is happening."

Chi Pan Ho threw a line across the bow of the explorer's ship and called, "Hoy, Ko Chan. We have come to rescue Prince Quai!"

"The imperial heir is in no danger; therefore, he requires no rescuing."

Ko Chan's answer enraged the pirate, who snatched up a line and swung from one vessel to the other. Drawing a dagger from his belt, he faced the explorer. "I want," he said, "Prince Quai."

To Ko Chan this was no longer a playful skirmish. "I know you well, Chi Pan Ho, and you'll dance on my sword's blade before I give up the Prince. Stand back, pirate!"

Chi Pan Ho, his chest glistening in the sun, snarled "Now thieves turn proud and call others names."

Sailors of the imperial navy stood firm, alert, as Ko Chan rushed toward the pirate. "Dare you call us thieves? I'll cut your mast in two myself!"

Chi Pan Ho, ignoring Ko Chan's sword, shoved the explorer's men aside and stood face to face with him. "Did you not make off with the Emperor's gold and silver bells as well as his son?"

"Gold and silver bells? I know only about the bells hanging on a tree in the Emperor's garden."

"The same," said the pirate giant. "It was discovered that they had been taken away after you had sailed. Only this vessel could have carried them away."

"Never!" snapped the angry explorer. "There are no imperial bells on board my barque."

Glee Mung, golden Princess of Kaesong, and wife of Ko Chan, leaned over the rail of the upper deck and asked, "Can these be some of the bells you speak of?" From her headdress she pulled three glittering objects and tossed them down at the feet of pirate and explorer.

"Bells—from the Emperor's tree!" sputtered Ko Chan. He looked up. "Where have you found them, Glee Mung?"

"They were in one of Prince Quai's sea chests. I found them there." The golden head tilted and mischief glittered in Glee Mung's eyes. "What I say is true."

Prince Quai, stunned by the sudden appearance of the bells, could only say, "I did not take them! I could not steal from my father."

Chi Pan Ho took advantage of Ko Chan's bewilderment. He moved in and separated the Prince from the explorer's men. "Come with me, Highness. The Princess lies to cover for Ko Chan's deceit." His thick left arm circled Prince Quai's shoulders.

But Ko Chan moved swiftly to cut off the pirate's retreat with the Prince. "Listen to me, Pirate!" commanded the explorer. "I will surrender to you if I find I have been deceived. If, on the other hand, this proves to be a plot to endanger the prince, I will cut off your ears and nail them to the deck. It will not take us long to discover who is being deceitful." He looked up to the golden Princess who still stood on the upper deck. "Tell me, Glee Mung, how did you know where to find the bells?"

The Princess wrinkled her nose and turned so that she looked down at Ko Chan over her shoulder. "A little shriveled man told me they would be my reward if I persuaded you to bring Prince Quai away from home."

"Sin Yang!" sputtered Ko Chan, spitting out the name in disgust.

"The same who bargained with me," said Chi Pan Ho, "to pursue you and force you to do battle. Then the fat treasure you carry would be mine!"

Men of the royal navy moved in, aiming to capture Chi Pan Ho. The pirate read the maneuver accurately and signalled his waiting cutthroats to swarm the deck of the royal barque.

"Pirate, help me!" shrieked Glee Mung. "Ko Chan will harm me, now that he knows. The bells will be yours if you save me!"

Pirates moved in to circle Ko Chan. Prince Quai jumped to the explorer's side. "Lend me a sword, Ko Chan," he begged. "Together we can hold them off!" Instead, Ko Chan forced the Prince to one side, then attacked the pirates fiercely, moving constantly to draw the fighting away from the imperial heir.

This tactic exasperated the hulking, sweating pirate chief. "Stand and be target. O swift of foot!" panted Chi Pan Ho. His muscles rippled in the sun as he sword flashed, slashed the air close to the explorer, then clanged against Ko Chan's blade, now rising in an upswing.

"So, you would cut me down and win the Princess of Kaesong for yourself!" taunted Ko Chan. He deftly sidestepped the pirate's glittering rapier.

"Exactly as Sin Yang promised!" Then, as Prince Quai moved in again to help the explorer, Chi Pan Ho warned him, "Back, Prince Quai! I have no mind to draw princely blood!"

Through the clanging of swords, Ko Chan called, "Bargain with me, Pirate! Take Kaesong and her bells; she begged your help. Leave me instead the Prince, who was put into my care by his father."

"Only if we return to China, I watching you and you watching me. And if we have been played off against each other, as you suspect, we will carve Sin Yang down the middle, together."

"Agreed!" shouted the explorer. He quickly laid his sword on the deck and stood, his arms spread wide, showing his hands empty of weapons.

Chi Pan Ho sheathed his own sword and saluted Ko Chan. Then he turned his attention to Glee Mung. "Princess, bring your bells and board my barque," he commanded.

Glee Mung scurried below decks to retrieve her chest of bells, then, reappearing, she hurried to Chi Pan Ho. She stooped and gathered up the little bells she had tossed, then signaled that she was ready for Chi Pan Ho to gather her up and swing her onto the pirate ship. As the transfer was made, Ko Chan shouted, "Pirate, I salute you! Let us sail quickly home to China."

But the return voyage was a long one, delayed by storms and glassy seas.

At home, the new set of bells was a well-kept secret. Each time they were hung, Reed Song read their message for the Emperor and Empress, but only when they knew the sinister Prime Minister was far away from the imperial garden.

One evening, after several months had passed, the Emperor found his Li Sung weeping. "Shed no tears for Quai, my dear one," he begged. "Our son is safe. This we know. Come. We will find Reed Song and carry the bells to the tree."

Li Sung sighed. "It is such a frail thread on which to build our hopes. Suppose Reed Song were lying, just to appease us?"

The Emperor took his wife's hand. "Can you think so little of the girl?"

The Empress followed docilely. Still, she said, "But if I were afraid of being punished, I would say I could understand the bells. Truly I would, Quo Ming."

The Emperor frowned at his wife's confession, then laughed

at the concept of an imperial fib. "Don't give it another thought," he advised. He led the Empress along familiar corridors until they reached the quarters of the maid of linens. He knocked on the door and called her name. "Reed Song? She does not answer." He lifted the latch and entered the maid's room. "She is not here," he reported as he stepped out again into the corridor. "The bells are not here. Reed Song has surely taken them to the garden."

"Oh, come quickly," murmured the Empress. "Perhaps she has a message."

Reed Song was at that moment hanging the bells, each in its proper place on the tree. Suddenly, Sin Yang appeared out of the shadows and came toward her.

"So, little one, you are here to try to speak with your tree again," he sneered. "What can it tell you without any—" Then he saw what Reed Song held in her hands. "Where did you get these bells? I gave them to the Princess of Kaesong! Has she returned them to the Emperor?"

Reed Song cowered in fright. "No. These are new bells. The Emperor has made a whole new set of bells."

Sin Yang moved quickly, to stand towering over the girl, a gleaming blade in one hand; he knit the fingers of his other hand into her hair. "The tree may speak, but you will not hear," he hissed. "And as for messages, my dagger will silence you and the tree."

Empress Li Sung, coming into the garden, saw at once what was happening. "No, no, Sin Yang," she screamed. "Free the girl! Do her no harm!"

"I do not choose to obey your imperial commands, Empress!" snorted the Prime Minister. "You cannot save the girl. She is all that stands between me and—but, that is another matter. She has meddled with my affairs, and she must pay for her meddling!" He pressed the dagger against Reed Song's throat.

The Emperor was startled to see other forms emerge from the shadows. He heard Reed Song scolding, "Take your hand from me, old man, or I shall be disrespectful and bite you!" She drew as far away from the dagger as she could.

The shadowy forms took shape as Sin Yang lunged again at Reed Song. "Little snippet! Your heart is my target!"

At that moment, Chi Pan Ho grasped the bony wrist of the Prime Minister. "Hold, old bag of bones! This is the Princess you promised me. You will use no dagger on her."

Sin Yang twisted round, trying to escape the massive hand, now recognizing who it was that held him. "Chi Pan Ho! Why are you not at sea?" Bewilderment flickered over the Prime Minister's face, but only for a moment. "Ho, guards! Seize this man!" he shouted. "He is a pirate!" And again he tried to squirm free.

Prince Quai, who had watched with horror Sin Yang's threatening gestures, moved quietly to his mother's side. When he touched her shoulder, she turned and, clutching him close, murmured, "Quai, you are safe!"

"I am, Mother. And I have won both pirate and explorer as friends and allies."

Ko Chan was next to emerge from the shadows. "I shall capture him for you, Sin Yang. But look, and he is already in my hand." Ko Chan with great ceremony laid his hand on Chi Pan Ho's, causing the giant to release Sin Yang, who repaid the explorer's kindness by attacking him with the dagger. Again Chi Pan Ho brought the Prime Minister under submission; still his dagger flailed the air, keeping the maid of linens from fleeing.

Ko Chan tried once more. "Here is one who can persuade you to release the girl—your friend, the Princess of Kaesong." He turned to Glee Mung who now showed every sign of fear. "Go to the old man, Glee Mung. If you will disarm him, I will take you back to Kaesong."

Cowering, Glee Mung refused. "I am afraid," she admitted. "He has a dagger, and he smells of death."

But Ko Chan was not convinced. "He cannot hurt you. Trade one of your bells for his dagger."

Trembling, the Princess of Kaesong approached Sin Yang. "Great statesman, old friend, I need a dagger like yours. I will give you this little silver bell for it." She held out the bell. "I helped you once. Will you help me now?"

Sin Yang turned to listen to Glee Mung. Indecisively, he held out the dagger. "But I must have a gold bell instead, or you may not have my dagger."

Meanwhile, pirate and explorer conferred. "Why not rush the old goat?" asked Chi Pan Ho. "I am quicker than he is. I can have that dagger out of his hand before he sees me."

"Creep up, round in back," urged Ko Chan.

The Tree of Bells jangled an urgent message and Reed Song, still in Sin Yang's grasp, cried out, "The Tree of Bells bids me warn you of your doom . . . Your neck will snap like a twig if you do not release me."

The crazed Prime Minister laughed at the tree's warning. From behind, Chi Pan Ho moved swiftly to wrap his arms around Sin Yang and lift him, kicking and squirming, from the ground. Suddenly, as Sin Yang twisted to try to see who held him, there was a loud cracking sound. His body went limp and his head dangled awkwardly over Chi Pan Ho's wrist.

"He—broke his own neck—here in my arms. I intended only to hold him as he held the girl."

The Empress and Quai moved into the open moonlight. "Come, stranger," commanded Li Sung. When he stood at her side, she said gently, "You could not prevent Sin Yang's death. We are grateful that you and the explorer have brought Prince Quai home safely. And even more grateful that you have saved Reed Song."

The Emperor watched as the pirate gently laid down the crumpled body of the Prime Minister. He shivered, realizing that the Tree of Bells had predicted all that had come to pass. "We must go in," said the Emperor. "The night is damp and cold. We shall have some food, and tea to warm us." He turned to the maid of linens. "Come along with us, Reed Song. Tonight you shall dine with the Prince."

Prince Quai took Reed Song's hand to lead her. "And you will be dining with the pirate and explorer who have rescued you. They are going to work together to build a new Ming navy, and I shall be its admiral."

The Tree of Bells chimed merrily, agreeing with Quai. And in the years that followed, the tree became a part of Old China, giving its friendly advice and music to all who would listen.

Two Buttons

The Days of Village Craftsmen

There was once a young cobbler who was called "Two Buttons" by his neighbors because he had the skill to make shoes fit comfortably even though they were fastened by only two buttons on each shoe. As often happened in the old days, the King of the land went on a pilgrimage Crusade to the Holy Land, leaving his people in the care of the Duke of Coldwater. The Duke, hitherto a kindly and generous man, soon became a cruel and tyrannical ruler who took the law into his own hands, sending home the Royal Judges and closing the Parliament, so that the pleas of the people would be heard by no one except the Duke himself. His position of power had gone to his head, much to the detriment of the populace.

Already he had doubled the taxes, and his most recent decree demanded triple tribute from each farmer and craftsman in the nation. It became the Duke's custom, and his chief source of amusement, to ride forth with his warden and his guards to each village, where he singled out one shop or place of business from which to collect the tax and tribute personally. And if the craftsman were unfortunate enough to be unable to pay on demand, the Duke himself beheaded the poor man, as an example to all others in that village. Needless to say, shopkeepers everywhere tried their best to have tax money on hand.

One bright morning, the Duke arrived at Trisket, the hamlet where Two Buttons dwelt. The village of Trisket hd been laid out long years ago by an ancestor of the Duke of Coldwater. There was a line of shops occupied by the craftsmen on one side of a fine stonecovered road and cartway, with a square village green on the other. Around the three sides of the green were built the cottages and houses where the families of the shopkeepers lived; the village church and churchyard were at one end of the side opposite the row of shops. A fine village it was, a model for others to follow, and already joined to the foot-and-horse pathway connecting to the King's Highway leading to the shire town.

The Duke's horsemen stopped at the bakery next door to the cobbler's shop, making such a disturbance that Two Buttons need not have put his ear to the wall to hear what was said.

"Your name and station?" demanded the Duke briskly.

"I'm Tim Wheatly, a baker by trade, your Honor."

The Duke's warden broke in to correct Tim with "your Highness," and Tim amended his answer with "your Highness."

"We find," said the Duke, "that last year you paid a mere five pounds, three shillings and fourpence in taxes, and only thirty loaves of bread in tribute. That will never do for this year. We'll set your tax at eleven pounds, and tribute at one hundred loaves. I propose to collect the tax now, and the tribute three months from now, there being enough bread in the ducal pantry to satisfy our needs for the time."

"But your Highness, I don't believe I have eleven pounds!" protested Tim. This brought such a howl of laughter from the guardsmen that Tim barely heard Two Buttons pounding on the wall. "What can Two Buttons want of me at a time like this?" wondered Tim. Then he said to the Duke, "Excuse me, your—Highness, I'll see what I can gather together to pay my tax; but I know I don't have that much money." Thereupon, he popped his head into the oven, as though to look for hidden funds. But this was how Tim Wheatly and Two Buttons talked with each other, for the wall of the oven reached into Two Buttons' shop, and a word spoken on either side was heard on the other.

"Don't worry me with your jokes, Two Buttons," Tim said. "I'm about to lose my head because I can't pay the Duke's tax."

"How much do you have to pay?" asked Two Buttons.

"Eleven pounds now, and a hundred loaves of bread later," came Tim's reply.

"Try to hold their attention, Tim my lad. Do them a dance, or sing them a little ditty; but keep them occupied, and I'll be back in quarter of an hour with your eleven pounds."

Tim banged shut the oven door. He did not doubt Two Buttons' good intentions, but he certainly couldn't expect the cobbler to succeed in finding the eleven pounds necessary to save Tim's head. Still, he did his best to keep the tax collectors happy. He brought out warm, fresh bread and offered it to the Duke and his guardsmen. They had come before breakfast to collect taxes from Trisket, and Tim saw the hungry gleam in their eyes as he sliced down the bread and set soft butter on the counter to go with it.

The Duke hesitated a moment, then nodded his approval and joined his men in enjoying Tim's simple feast. As they ate, Tim turned his attention to the search for odd pennies he had hidden here and there in the bakery.

Meanwhile, Two Buttons slipped quietly out of his shop, stole over to the Duke's horses, taking a saddle bag from one, the stirrups from another, and finally the saddle from the Duke's own mount. Hurrying away with these articles, Two Buttons ran from shop to shop, selling what he had for whatever he could get.

Paul the Binder and Edward the Dyer bought the stirrups and saddlebag, and Two Buttons came at last to the tannery owned by his old friend, Bruce. Here he beat upon the door to waken the elderly tanner. "Bruce, Bruce! Open to me! It's Two Buttons, and I must see you!"

Still rubbing sleep from his eyes, the old man lifted his latch and Two Buttons entered the shop. "Why do you disturb me, when I need my rest?" asked the old tanner.

"It's eternal rest for Tim the Baker, if I don't rouse Trisket. The Duke came calling with a demand for eleven pounds tax." Two Buttons paused to let Bruce understand that much. Then he went on. "Here is the Duke's saddle. What'll you give for it? Surely it's worth five pounds to you. See the inlay of silver? Where can you get such a bargain, Bruce?"

Still the old tanner did not comprehend. He blinked in the candlelight, licked his lips as he ran his hand over the saddle, but said nothing. Two Buttons tried to wake him.

"Come, Bruce—think! I've got six of the eleven pounds already. Paul the Binder and Edward the Dyer have bought of me, as has Peter the Potter. But I've saved the best for you—the Duke's own saddle, worth at least thirty pounds." Again Two Buttons waited.

"I have five pounds," Bruce admitted after half a minute. "But it's my tax money, laddie. What if the Duke comes calling on me?"

Two Buttons caught up the saddle and moved to the door. "Time enough to worry when he does. I have to hurry and find a buyer for the saddle. Will poor Tim lose his head for lack of five pounds?"

"Nawh," said Bruce as he dug under his apron and into his money pouch. "I'll not have it said I put myself before others. Here's the five pounds, and heaven rescue me when the tax collectors come."

Two Buttons swung the saddle up onto one of the shelves in the tanner's shop and collected the money. "Thanks, Bruce," he said. "You've struck a good bargain and saved a good man. I'll be back to tell you what happens."

In less than the quarter of an hour he had allowed himself for the task, Two Buttons was back in his shop. He dropped the money in an old pair of shoes, put them on the back stoop of the bakery, then pounded on the wall between the two shops.

Tim was still trying to keep the Duke's party contented when Two Buttons signaled his return. Tim turned again to the oven door, but the Duke's warden became suspicious and stopped him with "Here, here, what are you doing at that oven?"

Quickwitted, Tim replied, "I have to make sure the oven brick isn't cracked. I trust I can make certain that my shop is in good order before you behead me?" With a sneer the warden swaggered away and Tim climbed into the oven. "Have you had any luck?" he called through the oven wall.

Faintly he heard Two Buttons' reply:

On your back stoop you're bound to find
A pair of shoes. And if you're not blind,
In the left shoe you're going to see
The eleven pounds you asked of me.

"Oh, my goodness, you've succeeded!" Tim exclaimed, scrambling out of the oven and hurrying to the back door of the bakery. "Ah, here are the shoes. Will the coins add up? It's here; in copper and silver, but it's here!"

Tim bustled back into the shop, pretending to pick up a shilling here and a penny there. At last he approached the tax collector. "Oh great Duke, I can now pay my tax—every penny of the eleven pounds."

The Duke of Coldwater did not hide his disappointment at being denied an execution. He growled,
"You've taken long enough to gather it together!"

Tim, ever quick with his tongue, asked, "What's a poor baker to do? Leave his money around where any robber can find it easily?"

The Duke's warden took offense and grabbed Tim's collar. "Are you calling us robbers? I'll flog you for insulting us!"

But the Duke of Coldwater stopped the warden. "The man has paid his tax, Warden. We must go on to the next town before the sun rises high."

The Duke and his men stomped out of the bakery. Soon the cry went up: "These horses have been tampered with!" Saddle bags had been taken from horses ridden by the Duke's guards, and the warden found his tax records missing. But the Duke was in the greatest rage. "My saddle has been stolen! Call out the villagers! I'll flog them myself, every last one of them!"

The Duke's warden, relishing a campaign of cruelty, asked; "Shall I line them up in front of their cottages, your Highness?"

But the Duke saw that there would be too many residents of Trisket for his small party to handle. Hig anger cooled. As an alternative he snapped, "I can't spend all day in Trisket! But I have ways to even the score with these rabble. They will learn how foolish it is to steal a Duke's saddle."

The tax collectors mounted and road away, toward the King's highway, and the dwellers of Trisket tumbled into the street to learn what had happened.

Tim the Baker almost danced for joy. "Look! Here I am, with my head still on my shoulders. This calls for a celebration!"

From Edward the Dyer's cottage came Jenny, his daughter. "Tim! Tell us what has happened," she demanded.

"You'll have to ask Two Buttons," said Tim. "He did what was done."

Two Buttons sauntered from the doorway of his shop and Jenny turned to him saying, "Well then, Two Buttons, tell us."

"Not much to tell," replied Two Buttons. "The Duke came calling and collected Tim's taxes."

Todd the Tinker, hammer in hand, came up to pat Two Buttons on the back. " 'Twas a brave and fool-hardy trick, to steal the Duke's saddle."

Jenny clucked her tongue in dismay. "Oh, Two Buttons, how will you ever live long enough to become my husband?"

Two Buttons pinched Jenny's cheek. "Have no fear, Jenny love. It's only the good who die young. I'm fated to be an old man."

"And I'm fated to be an old maid if we don't marry soon," Jenny snapped.

Two Buttons took her in his arms and swung her off her feet. "Then Jenny, name the day," he said, "and we'll flout fate."

The villagers cheered at this and Libby, Jenny's mother, sighed, "At last—there's to be a wedding!"

Jenny was bubbling. "Next Thursday! No—we'll make it tomorrow!"

Libby sputtered at her daughter's impulsiveness. "Why, Jenny, you can't be ready that soon!"

"True, mother," admitted Jenny. "It'll have to be day after tomorrow."

"I'll bake the cake," Tim the Baker offered. "I'll start right away, Jenny. That's the least I can do, after Two Buttons' saving my neck."

Edward the Dyer, having stood quietly by, wiping green stains from his hands, came forward to Jenny and advised her, "Jenny, go in with your mother and sit down to plan your wedding. Take time to think. Then you'll know what's best."

"I will, Father," Jenny agreed, "if you bring Two Buttons home for tea."

"I'll come, Jenny, never fear," Two Buttons assured her. And then, as the women of Trisket turned back to their kitchens and the men were about to go to their shops, Two Buttons said quietly, "Let's meet in my shop this evening to have a word about what we can expect from his Highness, the Duke of Coldwater."

Edward the Dyer tugged at Two Buttons' sleeve. "Come along, man. The ladies will have tea ready."

Two Buttons turned away from the other men to follow Jenny's father. But at the cottage gate, Edward stopped him. "Since you're to be my son-in-law, don't you think you ought to ask for my daughter's hand?"

Two Buttons, suddenly confronted by the responsibility of speaking the traditional words, stammered and stuttered. "I—that is—could I have the honor?—may I presume to ask—?"

Edward the Dyer started to laugh. His round, fat shoulders shook and he pointed a fat finger at Two Buttons.

"Now, look here, Edward the Dyer!" sputtered Two Buttons.

But Edward roared his hearty "Ho, ho! Wait til I tell Jenny you can't even ask me!"

Two Buttons was terrified. "You wouldn't tell her that,

now, would you?"
"If I had a mind to, son." But now Edward stopped his teasing. "Let's say that I'll gladly give you my daughter if you promise to be a good and faithful husband to her."

"I'll work at it all my life," Two Buttons promised as he swung open the gate.

When they entered the cottage, Edward's wife Libby bustled them into comfortable chairs by the fire. "You men have been so long," she fretted, "that the tea's stone cold. Jenny, be a dear and go brew some fresh."

"Yes, Mother," said Jenny, and she obediently went about doing the chore set for her.

Edward warmed his hands by the fire. "Libby," he asked, "haven't you a word for your daughter's intended?"

Libby came close to the handsome cobbler and put a loving hand on his shoulder. "I have more than a word for you, Two Buttons. Jenny has feathers for brains this day and I don't know what she'll be like by your wedding day, but you know I've counted you as good as my son for a long time."

Two Buttons looked up to Libby, surprised by this show of affection. Edward chuckled. "Surprised are you? That's the woman's way of it, my lad. We're both glad to have you joining the family."

"But why couldn't you have let Jenny set the day six months ago?" Libby asked. "She'll burn the candle all night, sewing on her wedding dress. You men make such sudden decisions!"

Edward interceded for Two Buttons. "Now, Mother, the boy's not to be scolded two days before his wedding. You know you sewed on your wedding dress the night before we were married. All girls do it." Edward grinned over his profound pronouncement.

Now Jenny came, carrying a tray heaped high. "Tea's ready, Mother," she said, "and I've brought more cakes."

"Then pour the tea and pass the cakes, Jenny, that's a dear." Libby clucked her tongue. "I really don't know how we'll manage by day after tomorrow."

Jenny comforted her mother with "Don't worry, Mother. I'll sew all night, if I have to." Then she turned to the man who was soon to be her husband. "What's the matter, Two Buttons? You haven't said a word."

Two Buttons lifted his shoulders in an expression of hopelessness. "I've been trying to think how to save my neck," he explained, "if the tax and tribute are demanded of me tomorrow. I have half a crown for the priest who marries us, Jenny, but not a penny for the Duke."

After supper that evening, the craftsmen of Trisket gathered about the cobbler's bench in Two Buttons' place of business.

"There was blood in his eye, when the Duke rode away," said Paul the Binder, exulting in the Duke's rage.

"But they'll be back, mark my words," warned Edward the Dyer.

"Then we must be ready for them," said Tim Wheatly, the baker, resolutely. "If Two Buttons hadn't helped me today, I'd be without my head now." Tim rubbed his neck appreciatively.

"Fine enough to say we must be ready for the Duke and his men. We don't know who of us will be next, or we could see that he has the money to pay his tax." Bruce, the old harness maker, took another draw on his pipe. "That's if we've got the money between us."

"Let's not be downhearted," urged Peter the Potter.

"All well enough to say, 'don't be downhearted,' " muttered Bruce. "I had five pounds to pay my taxes, but now all I own is a saddle decorated with silver."

"Don't talk like that," insisted Peter. "You've never had such a bargain, Bruce. Why, I have a cousin in the big city who will be glad to pay you three times that for such a fine piece of workmanship."

"Aye, but what good will that do me, if the Duke comes to my door tomorrow? Could I trade his saddle in payment for my taxes?" Bruce chuckled and the craftsmen of Trisket laughed with him over the ridiculous suggestion, but they knew the situation was far from funny.

Two Buttons spoke up to assure Bruce. "There will be a way to help you, Bruce. What we must work out is a plan that will protect all of us."

"Of a certainty," said optimistic Peter. "When the Duke walks into your shop, tap on the wall and call for Two Buttons. The man in the next shop will pass the word along until Two Buttons hears. Then he can come along the alleyway to see what can be done. If anyone can outwit the Duke, it's Two Buttons."

Bruce knocked the ash from his pipe and agreed. "Aye. He's as good as any three of us."

Two Buttons knew that luck had played a great part in the successful conclusion of today's adventure, and he certainly could not allow all of Trisket to depend upon him alone. So he asked, "But what happens if the Duke comes to my shop? Do I knock on the wall and pass the word to myself?"

Todd the Tinker had been idly handling one of the hammers on Two Buttons' bench. Now he slammed it down with a thump. "If you cannot figure a way out of that predicament, then we're all doomed."

Two Buttons took up his hammer and laid it in its proper place. "My friends," he said, "we gain nothing by looking only on the dark side of this situation. We have to be alert and aware of what is happening at all times, especially when the Duke and his men are in Trisket. One and all must work together to outwit the troublemakers. They are intent on one thing: to bring misery to otherwise happy people. They concentrate on that purpose so hard that they make mistakes—they leave loopholes through which we can slip. How can we find those loopholes unless we remain calm and avoid the panic of frightened rabbits?"

Howard the Miller, imbued with his superiority to the other men of Trisket, and usually haughty and aloof, had, nonetheless, graced the meeting with his presence. Now he spoke up: "It seems to me that the Duke would be far more forgiving and, yes, reasonable if his property had not been stolen. That, I believe, was a fatal error in judgment. I think we must question it seriously."

Several of Trisket's craftsmen muttered against Howard's criticism, but Two Buttons answered him squarely. "The theft of the Duke's saddle was a dangerous gesture—foolhardy, perhaps, but necessary. I chose to take the saddle to make the Duke uncomfortable, to make him realize that he cannot terrorize the people of Trisket or bully us into submission. If the day comes when we cannot meet his demands, I will surrender myself to take the place of anyone the Duke threatens to behead. Until then, we must all keep ready to help each other, to give what we have for the good of all."

The good craftsmen of Trisket saw the wisdom of Two Buttons' suggestion and agreed to be on the alert, ready to do what was needed when next the Duke of Coldwater came to collect taxes.

Next morning, the Duke and his party rode up to Peter the Potter's shop. Two Buttons, watching from his own window, did not wait for a signal but instead went flying along the rear of the row of shops, arriving at the pottery in time to hear Peter shriek "Fourteen pounds! I paid only five pounds last year!"

Peering cautiously through the rear window, Two Buttons saw the swaggering Duke stride back and forth, waving his riding whip. "The extra tax will excuse you from tribute," said the Duke with a sneer. "We need no more dishes at the palace—don't know what to do with what we have!" And he went on thrashing about Peter's shop, frightening the potter out of his wits.

"Poor Peter!" thought Two Buttons. "He's counting on me to help him. I hope I can."

Two Buttons turned first to Paul the Binder, next door to the pottery. Paul, a tall, thin young fellow, was bent over his huge vise, sewing a binding, when Two Buttons burst in. He was so intent on his work that he had not heard the commotion in the road or through the shop walls.

"You know why I've come to you," Two Buttons whispered. "Give with generous fingers, Paul."

"Who is it today?" asked the binder.

Two Buttons patted the wall between the shops. "It's Peter who is honored."

Paul dug into his money bag and hurriedly counted out coins. "Three sovereigns is all I have, but you're welcome to them."

"Thanks," said Two Buttons, scooping up the money. He strode quickly out of the bindery and on to Todd the Tinker's workroom. The door was barred and Two Buttons had to knock and call out in a hoarse whisper, "Todd, let me in! it's Two Buttons!"

The tinker pulled back the bar and cautiously opened the door. "Be quick, man," sputtered Two Buttons, brushing past the squat little tinsmith. "Get out your money—all of it. Peter has to have fourteen pounds or Trisket loses its potter."

Todd turned his back to Two Buttons, shielding with his shoulder the hiding place he used for his funds. "I should have been a coiner instead of a tinker," he said.

"If worse comes to worst, we'll put you to making tin sovereigns for his Highness, the Duke." They both laughed, pleased by the thought.

"May these be a weight around his neck!" prayed Todd as he placed all his coins in Two Buttons' hands.

Once again in the street, the cobbler wondered where to turn next. "Bruce has nothing but the Duke's saddle, and the brewer is sick-a-bed. Will the Weaver bought three bags of wool last week, using what he had put by in the way of money. I'd best go directly to my father-in-law-to-be. Howard the Miller would only tell me what I should have done. The Duke must be very impatient by now."

He scurried past the brewer, the tanner and the weaver to Edward the Dyer's shop. "I'm sorry to rob my bride of her dowry," he said, "but if I must, I must." He knocked at the door of Edward's shop. "It's Two Buttons, Edward."

The dyer's door swung open. "How much do you need this time, lad?" He beckoned to Two Buttons to come in.

"I have only six pounds," Two Buttons explained," and Peter has to pay fourteen."

"I think I can just make it," said Edward, wiping the moist dye from his hands, "but it will take the last of my silver."

"I'd have stopped at Will the Weaver's—."

"You did right in coming to me. Will has laid out his reserve for new wool." Edward the Dyer laid out eight shining sovereigns on the drainboard of his purple dye vat and Two Buttons expressed his thanks as he picked them up. Then off he hurried with the tax money for Peter the Potter.

"Now how can I get the money into Peter's hands without the Duke being any the wiser about what we're doing here in Trisket?" As Two Buttons entered Peter's back yard, he saw a tub of slurry water. "And Peter has a lump of clay soaking in it. That will do nicely," said Two Buttons. He pulled the soft mass out of the slurry water and imbedded the coins he had gathered in the lump of clay, then rushed into the pottery shop with it.

"Here are the fourteen pounds of clay you shouted for, Peter. I brought it as fast as I could. Knowing you have important visitors, I'll not take up your time." Two Buttons winked and started for the door.

"Than—thanks, Two Buttons. I—" stammered Peter.

"Not another word, man. Get on with your business before the clay dries." Two Buttons was already on his way to the door.

"I'll dance at your wedding and sing at your wake!" promised Peter. Then he turned to the Duke, who was fuming over the delay. "If your Grace will be patient, just a moment. I must cover the clay before it sets too firmly for working."

"Go on, go on," growled the Duke. "Then you must hand over your tax money. I haven't all day!"

Two Buttons had hurried from the pottery, along the street to the corner and around into the alley. When he reached the back window of Peter's shop, he watched the anxious potter pull the coins from the lump of clay. When he saw all fourteen pounds in Peter's hand, Two Buttons scurried back to his own shop and pounded happily on a pair of shoes.

When evening came the villagers gathered on the green before Edward the Dyer's house to dance and celebrate the Wedding Eve of Jenny and Two Buttons. Will the Weaver and Paul the Binder set up a long trestle table alongside the footpath. Their wives spread a snowy cloth on the table and from the cottages came other women to cover it with plates of meat pies, cheese, small cakes and fruit. Jack Alemaster, the brewer, trundled a barrow holding a half-keg of ale across the commons from the brewery and Peter the Potter set out new mugs as his part of the happy celebration. A bonfire, built on the green for this special occasion, was now lighted, to cheers from the crowd.

Nearly all the residents of Trisket were on hand for the festivities. Howard the Miller and his wife Margaret were too haughty and self-important to be seen at so common an affair as a Wedding Eve celebration. However, it was well understood that the miller and his family would grace the ceremony with their presence on the morrow. Howard, as church warden, must attend the service and sign the parish register to record the marriage.

Ben the Blacksmith beat on a tambourine and Anna, his wife, sang tunes for the dancing, and many there were who joined in the jolly time. But soon there were calls for "The Bride! Let us see the Bride! We have cakes and ale for a toast to the Bride!"

And of course that was just the cue Jenny and her mother Libby had been waiting for. Libby threw open the door and Jenny skipped out, dropped a curtsy at the gate, and danced into the center of the circle of villagers who sang and clapped rhythmically as she whirled round and round. Will the Weaver threw more wood on the bonfire and it burned more brightly as everyone sang happily:

Jenny is the Bride-O Bride-O, Bride-O!
Jenny is the Bride-O, Tomorrow is the day!
Jenny to the Church-O, Church-O, Church-O!
Jenny to the Church-O, the Priest will have his say!

When the bride's health had been drunk for the fifth time, as well as an equal number of toasts to the groom, the women of Trisket crowded into Edward the Dyer's house where Libby and Jenny displayed the contents of Jenny's hope chest and other fine presents for the soon-to-be-wed couple.

Meanwhile, it did not take the menfolk long to draw off to one corner of the village green where they discussed the day's happenings.

Peter the Potter was happy and excited over his escape from the Duke's wrath. "Oh, was I ever glad to see you this morning, Two Buttons! The Duke was mad as a hornet when I produced the tax payment. I think he's beginning to be suspicious of our conspiracy. He wants a beheading in Trisket to teach us a lesson. But, thanks to Two Buttons, my friends, I wasn't the victim!"

"Don't be too sure you're safe, Peter," snapped Two Buttons. "If worse comes to worst, we'll send you out to peddle Bruce's saddle to the Duke himself, instead of your cousin in the big city." The mug he threw down smashed at Peter's feet. "It's not I who has saved you! Our friends have given all they have to hold off the Duke. You have no right to crow when there's no money left to save the next man honored with a ducal visit."

Peter's smile faded from his face and joy was gone from his voice when, after a dreadful silence, he spoke. "I'm truly sorry, Two Buttons. I didn't mean to crow. I'll make amends."

Awkwardly, Paul the Binder put a friendly hand on Peter's shoulder. "That's all right, Peter. Any one of us would be as giddy if we had escaped the Duke's axe this morning."

"I agree with Peter in this," said Tim Wheatly. "The Duke of Coldwater wants to punish Trisket for the loss of his fine saddle. We can't be too careful—and we can't have a falling-out among friends. We're all in this together."

"You are right, Tim," said Two Buttons. "I'm sorry I gave Peter so much rough tongue. It's just that I've been trying so hard to come up with an idea of what to do next."

"Well, then, what are we to do?" Tim asked.

Two Buttons carefully picked up the shards of the broken mug. "First," he said, "let us try to discover how the Duke decides which of us he will honor with a visit." By the light of the bonfire, he arranged the broken pieces in a row along the top of the stone fence. "My shop's on the corner. The Duke did not come there. He skipped me but went instead to Tim, next door to me. Today he didn't go next door to Tim. He skipped Todd the Tinker and Paul the Binder, and entered Peter the Potter's shop." Two Buttons fingered the broken bits of pottery as he spoke. "So far, it has been: 'Skip one; skip two.' If that pattern is repeated, the next to meet the Duke is Bruce. But the next step may be 'Skip three.' That would be Edward the Dyer's."

Bruce the Tanner clapped his hands to his head. "If the Duke comes to me, there'll be a beheading for certain!"

"Not on my wedding day, there won't," declared Two Buttons. "I have something in mind, Bruce, whether he chooses you or Edward. But I see the women are coming back from Libby's parlor; it's best that we return to the dancing."

As the men started across the common, Two Buttons put his hand on Edward the Dyer's arm. "I'd like a word with you, Father-in-law, if you don't mind."

Edward grinned. "Are you getting nervous about tomorrow, son?"

"No," replied Two Buttons, "but we must prepare in case the Duke pays us another visit tomorrow."

Edward sputtered. "But it's your wedding day, man. You'll have to let someone else worry about the Duke!"

"I'd like to," said Two Buttons, "but it seems I'm the only one who can do what's got to be done. Now if the Duke comes to you tomorrow, I want you to take him into the vat room and show him your purple dye. Leave everything else to me. Just find some excuse to coax the Duke into the vat room."

Edward was impressed with his young friend's request. "I'll do what you say, but I can't see what good it will do."

By the light of the bonfire Edward saw a sad and weary expression cover Two Buttons' face. The cobbler sighed. "You have trusted me many times before this; will you trust me now? And no matter what happens tomorrow, tell Jenny not to worry. You'll do that for me?"

Edward gave Two Buttons his hand. "That I will, son." Then, noticing Jenny standing alone beside the table, he added, "The girl is waiting to dance with you. Go to her."

Two Buttons needed no urging, for now his mind was clear of doubts about tomorrow. He stood before his bride-to-be and begged, "Dance with me, Jenny?"

Jenny laughed a girlish laugh and took his hand. "For always, Two Buttons," she promised. And as they danced, she teased him, asking "Oh, what will my name be? Will it be Jenny Allen, which is your proper name—or Jenny Two Buttons?"

"I'll call you Jenny Mine, or Jenny Love, or any Jenny you want to be called," he promised.

"I want everyone to call me Jenny Two Buttons, but you may call me anything you wish."

Two Buttons laughed and whirled her around. "Perhaps I'll name you Old Boots or Broken Heel."

Jenny stamped her foot. "No! Nor Loose Tongue, either! I'll be Jenny Two Buttons or nothing!"

They spun away across the green, then close to the bonfire where, not caring who saw, they kissed each other goodnight a dozen times.

Bright and early the next morning Two Buttons, after a good night's sleep, sat in his shop doorway, wide awake and watching for the Duke and his guardsmen to ride into town. Sure enough, the five horses were reigned to a halt before Edward the Dyer's shop.

Two Buttons could hear the cries of confusion as he sped around the corner and along the rear of the shops. "Skip three! I haven't a moment to spare. If only the door to Edward's vat room is open! And it is—and there's the vat of purple dye. The drainboard will give me enough space to hide in its shadow. I've only time to plunge in!" Two Buttons dropped into the warm purple dye; he spashed the liquid over his head and face. "How strong it smells. But Edward is famous for his long-lasting dyes. Footsteps coming? Ah, we're in luck! Edward has persuaded the Duke to come to see the vats!" Sucking in a vast gulp of air, Two Buttons plunged under the surface of the dye.

Edward had, indeed, convinced the Duke that he really must see why the dyer was so well-known and prosperous. "I've always wanted to show a member of royalty how I achieve the beautiful shade of purple they love so well. If your Grace will step this way? A little closer and you will see the shreds of wood I use to make the dye fast."

The Duke, feigning high good humor, swaggered up to the drainboard of the purple dye vat. As he leaned over the edge, a purple hand grasped his wrist and, as he toppled, another took hold of his ankle and the Duke—hat, boots, and all—plunged into the purple dye.

Edward stood frozen with horror by what he saw happening before his eyes. There was a noiseless thrashing about in the vat, a few gurgles and some bubbling before he heard a raging voice bellow, "Get me out of here!"

The spell broken, Edward went stumbling from the vat room into the shop. "Help! Guardsmen!" he wailed. "The Duke has fallen into one of my dye vats!"

Thus alerted, the guardsmen pushed by the dyer. They snarled as purple dye splashed over them while they lifted a dripping, storming Purple Duke from the vat. Two Buttons, wearing the Duke's soggy, now-purple doublet and dribbling, misshapen hat, bellowed in a voice imitating the Duke's, "Flog him! No, no! take me back to the palace! I shall come tomorrow to flog him myself!"

"Oh, your Grace," Edward cried in abject apology, "such a thing has never happened before."

Two Buttons turned to face Edward, but his wink was lost on the terrified dyer. "You let me fall into that dye vat," he shouted, "and I will take it out on your hide. And it had to be fast dye! It will never come off!"

The guardsmen, under direction from the Duke's warden, hurriedly mopped the moisture from the Duke's face. There he stood, dyed from head to toe a magnificent royal purple. Edward huddled into a corner of his shop as the Duke stamped about, shaking the wet dye from his plumed hat, all the while ranting about the way he had been treated in Trisket.

There was no placating him, and on the way back to the ducal palace, he vented his wrath on each man in turn. Because of this, the guards were reassured that the Duke had suffered no great injury. As Edward the Dyer has assured him, the dye was fast, and it was many a day before it began to wear off.

Meanwhile, back in Trisket, Peter the Potter was searching for Two Buttons. After his encounter with the Duke, Edward had hurriedly closed the dye shop and gone home. Still trembling with fright, Edward could scarcely answer when Peter asked, "Where is Two Buttons, Edward? He has to dress for the wedding."

"I haven't seen him since last night, Peter. With all this excitement caused by the Duke's visit, I haven't had a chance to go see him."

"The word has gone round that the Duke has a lasting souvenir of his visit to your shop—and that's one for you, Edward!"

"Aye, but the score will be against me when the Duke returns with his axe."

Peter stopped to consider, then he said, "I saw Two Buttons go in the back door of your vat room this morning a short while before the commotion started. Look you! Here comes Tim, carrying the wedding cake."

Edward hurried to swing open the gate for Tim. "Tim, lad, have you seen Two Buttons?" he asked as he guided the baker into the parlor.

"He's been up to some foolishness, I've no doubt," Tim said as he settled the cake carefully on the table in the center of the room. "Why I don't know, but I saw him go into the back of your shop."

"But he's not been within my sight since last night," sputtered Edward, "Not since he told me to show the Duke my purple dye vat." A puzzled look spread over the dyer's face as Peter the Potter crowed, "Good for Two Buttons! He could have pushed the Duke into the vat. But it's not like Two Buttons to run and hide after he's played one of his tricks."

"Perhaps he met with an accident," suggested Tim Wheatly.

Now Edward was genuinely worried. "Let us go see," he said. "The poor lad may be lying in agony, with a broken leg."

"More than likely you've locked him in the shop after all the excitement," suggested Peter.

"I hope it's only that," said Edward. They hurried across the village green to the dyer's shop, Edward and Peter and Tim. As Edward threw open the door to the vat room, they all three cried out in dismay as they saw a man's body floating on the surface of the purple dye.

There was agony in Tim's voice. "Two Buttons! He's drowned, the poor fellow. He who saved me from the Duke!"

"And me, too, he saved," added Peter sorrowfully.

There was much splashing and huffing and puffing as the three craftsmen hauled the dead man from the dye vat. So upset were they that they thought nothing of finding Two Button's clothes floating free of the body.

"Dear, dear, dear!" wailed Edward. "Today was to be his wedding day, and now he's drowned, trying to save me! Did I tell you that his last words to me were 'Tell Jenny that everything will be all right'? Here, help me pull on his breeches. 'Twouldn't be right to have anyone see him naked."

The other two lent a hand, and in a short time the dead man was dressed in Two Buttons' clothing. "Now there will be no one to stand between us and the Purple Duke," was Peter the Potter's lament as he pulled on the left shoe.

But Tim the Baker was thinking about someone else. "Poor Jenny! A widow before she's married!"

"Lift him gently, the poor man!" said Edward.

It was Peter the Potter who now took charge. "We'll carry him to his own shop. He's purple from head to toe, like the Duke. I can hardly recognize him, but that's his jacket." Peter rolled the body from side to side, pulling dripping sleeves over purple arms. "I'll bring a rack from my kiln—"

And then came a voice from beyond the vat room. It was the bride-to-be, Jenny. "Father, where are you?" she called. "It's time you came home to dress for my wedding."

"Jenny, girl, don't come near!" Edward shouted. "Stay out in the shop." And then he added, "Go home! Go home!"

But Jenny was not to be deterred. She came bustling into the vat room, declaring "This is my wedding day and you must close the shop." She halted at the dead man's feet. "Oh, father, what have you there?" she cried in horror. "It's a man! And he's —." Her wail of sorrow filled the vat room.

"Yes, girl," said Edward. "You wouldn't go home, like I told you. Now you see for yourself: it's Two Buttons, drowned trying to save your father from the Duke. Now there's no husband for you, and no one to protect Trisket. Call the craftsmen together, lass. Have them meet in Two Buttons' shop, so we can do things right for Two Buttons."

Jenny hurried away, carrying her sorrowful message throughout the village while her father and Peter and Tim carried the dead man to the cobbler's shop.

When the Purple Duke returned to Trisket the next morning, he found the shops draped in black banners, and the whole village in mourning for Two Buttons. Edward the Dyer sat listlessly on the stoop in front of his shop.

"What is the matter here?" asked the Purple Duke.

"One of our shopkeepers has died," Edward reported sorrowfully. "We found him drowned in my vat of purple dye—the one you . . . fell into."

The Purple Duke laughed at Edward's discomfort. "What? Twice in one day? My man, you should be more careful in your dyeing."

"He was to be my son-in-law," Edward explained, "and my poor daughter is weeping in her bed."

Two Buttons, seeing that he must carry through his masquerade, at least for now, said, "I intended flogging you for your discourtesy to me yesterday. But here's a little money: see that the poor fellow has a decent burial." Two Buttons patted Edward's shoulder with a very purple hand and added, "And tell your daughter that everything will be all right."

Edward, beginning to recognize the voice and remembering those exact words, guessed, "Why—you must be—Two Buttons!" Then, reproachfully, he asked, "How can you do this to Jenny?"

Two Buttons shook his purple head and said regretfully, "I'm sorry for Jenny, Father, but it was the only way I could see of stopping the Duke from tormenting Trisket.

"Do for him as you would for me, Edward. Then take each shop keeper aside and tell him what you know. And be very gentle when you tell Jenny. I'm guilty of doing something terribly wrong to stop another from doing something terribly wrong. She may never forgive me."

Edward wept at the sorry plight of the young cobbler. "Two Buttons," he said, "you have much work to do, to undo the wickedness of the Duke of Coldwater. And you have a difficult part to play. Go back to the palace and do your best. I will take care of what must be done here."

Lonely and alone, the Purple Duke returned to the ducal palace and called his warden and guardsmen together. "We must leave the people of Trisket at peace," he said. "Who was to know our visits to collect the King's taxes would lead to the shoemaker's death? We must lie low for some time."

The Duke's warden, amazed by this change of tactics, asked, "But, your Grace, who will collect the taxes if we don't?"

The Duke strode haughtily to the window, looked out, and then said, "It is perfectly clear that we can collect no more taxes. That is a problem for His Majesty. It wouldn't do to have the King hear of our—escapade—or we'll lose our heads when he returns to the country."

The warden had never heard the Duke of Coldwater reason in this manner. He could not understand why the Purple Duke would make a decision so thoroughly out of character with his earlier plan of action. The warden stamped one foot, then the other, rubbed his chin and finally suggested, "There may be another solution to the problem, your Grace."

"No, no," insisted the Purple Duke, "it is best this way." He tossed his plumed hat onto the table in a gesture of contempt. "Pay the men from the treasury, Warden—and take as much as you need for yourself."

"Very well, your Grace," conceded the suspicious warden. "Guardsmen, you will assemble in the great hall to receive your pay." And with that, they marched out, leaving the Purple Duke alone.

Upon being paid off, the guardsmen dispersed to their homes, happy to enjoy their furlough. But the Duke's warden, sullen over his degrading dismissal and worse, losing his important command, became more and more suspicious of the Duke's change of heart. Therefore, he sent a message to the king, spelling out his suspicions and his anxiety over the suspension of collecting the King's taxes.

Meanwhile, over the next several weeks, the Purple Duke had fits of loneliness, and frequently he was seen to visit the shopkeepers of Trisket. On one such occasion, he went to see Peter the Potter.

"Two Buttons! Your Grace! Come in!" sang Peter. "Jenny's here, waiting for you."

From behind a rack of bowls and plates came Jenny. She dropped a curtsy appropriate for the ducal presence, then skipped over to throw her arms around the Purple Duke. "Oh, my Purple Duke!" she cried. "You're fading! Whatever will you do?"

Two Buttons picked up Jenny and carried her out into the sunlit road. "Jenny, love, we'll go swim in your father's dye vat. Then we'll both be purple!"

"No, no!" shrieked Jenny. "Set me down, you lout. Do you want the whole village talking about us?"

As they walked along the edge of the village green, Two Buttons asked, "Are you still sewing on your wedding dress?"

Jenny swung her bonnet by its strings. "You must not tease, Two Buttons," she said seriously.

"I know," said Two Buttons. "No matter what excuse I make for it, I have to admit I killed a man, and now my punishment is that I must live in his shoes, his clothes, and his palace—and he lies in my grave in the churchyard."

As it happened, the Duke's warden had taken to spying on the Purple Duke. A week before, he had summoned several dependable members of the guard and had chosen this very afternoon to trail the Purple Duke to Trisket. On foot, the warden and his four henchmen crept along the edge of the woods behind cottages, and followed Jenny and Two Buttons back to the shops.

The men of Trisket gathered before Peter the Potter's place of business. One and all greeted the Purple Duke as their old friend, the cobbler, Two Buttons. Even Howard the Miller, usually too busy to pass the time of day with the other craftsmen, came over to exchange a word or two with the purple one, slapping him jovially on the back and exclaiming, "You really must come to supper with Margaret and me one of these days, Two Buttons. We've always been fond of you, man, and now that you have assumed a position of importance—."

The Duke's warden and his henchmen huddled at the edge of the wood, listening and spying. "Listen to them!" rasped the warden. "Do you hear? They call him Two Buttons, the name of the cobbler who drowned in the dye vat."

One of the guardsmen asked, "Are you saying that the Duke is really the cobbler?"

"That's what I'm saying. The Duke of Coldwater has been slain and an imposter now masquerades as the Duke. Have you not seen the change in his habits, what he says and does? Have you not seen the change in his attitude toward Trisket, and even toward his responsibility to the King?"

"Aye," replied the guardsmen as one man.

"Let me tell you, I have sent a letter to the King, explaining my suspicions, and asking for his attention to the curious matter of a greatly changed Duke of Coldwater. But our crusading Majesty cares little for what happens here at home. It is up to us to avenge the Duke. When we move in, I want you to surround the purple one, so that his friends cannot help him. Then, leave me to deal with him."

They spent a long, breathless, hot half hour, watching for the best opportunity to catch the men of Trisket off guard. "I think there will be a new Duke of Coldwater when the King hears of our work here today," muttered the warden. Then he gave the signal: "Now!"

There were cries of anguish as the guardsmen moved in quickly to isolate the Purple Duke and cut off his escape.

"Ho! Great Purple Duke!" shouted the warden. "I have come in the name of the King to take vengeance on you!"

Jenny, who had been sitting quietly on the stoop in front of her father's shop, began to scream in terror when she saw her Two Buttons surrounded by guardsmen. Her screams brought many of the women of Trisket hurrying unto the village green, the little children hanging to their mothers' skirts.

"I believe you are an imposter," spat the warden venomously, "and it pleases me to challenge you to swords. If, indeed, you be the Duke of Coldwater, you can slay me in an instant. But if you are the cobbler, Two Buttons, as I suspect, you know nothing of swords and will quickly meet the end you deserve!" He flicked his blade, and it flashed in the sunlight.

"Stand back! Stand back!" warned the guardsmen. "Make room for swordplay!" In the middle of the stone-covered road, they pulled back into a semicircle behind the warden while the people of Trisket withdrew to a safe distance behind Two Buttons.

"I am without a weapon," said Two Buttons. "I left my sword in the palace."

"Then you shall have mine, and I'll use one from the guards!" shouted the warden. He sent his sword sailing through the air, into Two Buttons' hand, and then he accepted a replacement from the closest of his henchmen.

From the shadows stepped a tall, muscular man, clad in black and wearing a helmet of silver and leather. "Hold your blade, Challenger," he said. "A man may still have a champion!"

The guardsmen rushed to the warden's side, but the man in the helmet sang out: "Stand back, all of you! I will fight for the Purple Duke!" Taking the warden's sword from Two Buttons, the stranger in black strode to the center of the road. There was nothing for the warden to do but raise his borrowed rapier as the stranger barked out, "On guard!"

The villagers drew back to the edge of the green. "A champion—an unknown champion," they murmured.

"Where have you come from, Helmeted One?" called Jenny.

"That you will soon learn, my lady."

The Duke's warden parried and lunged, but his adversary was far more adept in handling a sword. As he drove the warden back, step by step, he said, "I have been following you and your guards for two days, and I have learned that you have ambitions which I must challenge!"

Insulted, the warden bellowed with rage and drove forward with his blade. The duel which followed was sharp and skillful, each swordsman using his cleverest thrusts and parries. The simple folk of Trisket, not daring to cheer when the champion seemed to gain the upper hand, stood silently watching, fearful that the ruthless warden might still cut down the stranger.

But at last the man in black gained vantage over the warden and, with a flick of the sword, wounded him. As the warden staggered in pain, the victor stood back and ordered, "Guardsmen, bind the warden's wounds. I have no wish to kill a subject of the King!" With that, the swordsman whisked off his helmet and everyone in the crowd recognized their crusading King.

Jenny, who had been clinging to Two Buttons during the duel, dropped a deep curtsy and murmured, "Your Majesty."

The King turned to her and said, "Do not be frightened, young lady, either for your Two Buttons or yourself. I have been in the country, home from my crusade for a month now, and I have learned of the cruelty displayed by him who was the Duke of Coldwater."

Two Buttons, still the Purple Duke, stepped forward and declared, "I am ready to acknowledge my guilt, your Majesty. I must confess that, when the opportunity came, I drowned the cruel Duke in the vat of purple dye, and then saw that I could undo some of his mischief by taking his place as the Purple Duke. I am ready to accept your judgement and verdict, my King."

His Majesty considered for a moment. "It is true that two wrongs do not make a right. I cannot say that I would not have done what you did, had I been in your place. Therefore, be it known that I hereby pardon Two Buttons of his offenses."

Jenny, forgetting royal dignity, flung her arms around the King. "Oh, for that, thanks, thanks great King! He did only what he thought best for the people."

"Aye, Jenny's right!" shouted Paul the Binder.

"I know," said the King. He turned to Jenny. "I have

learned of your sad wedding day, Jenny. But I cannot give you back your Two Buttons. I need him as the Duke of Coldwater."

There was a great shout of approval from the residents of Trisket. Two Buttons knelt at the King's feet. His Majesty touched the cobbler on both shoulders with the warden's sword and commanded, "Rise, Allen, Duke of Coldwater!"

Looking up, the Purple Duke said, "Thank you for my life, your Majesty, and for this honor which you have given me."

The King put out his hand and urged the new Duke to his feet. "As a loyal subject of the crown, you have defended the people against tyranny, Sir Allen. May you always serve so noble a purpose!" He smiled as he turned to Jenny. "And I hope he has enough sense to make you his Duchess without delay."

Jenny blushed prettily and turned away from the King. Two Buttons pursued her to the edge of the crowd of townsmen who closed in around the King with questions about his crusading.

Two Buttons put his arm around Jenny. "Come, love, tell me, will you be my Duchess?" And when she nodded her head, he asked, "And when will the wedding be?"

Looking up at her Purple Duke, Jenny said, "I don't know when I'd be ready—to marry a Duke. Next week? Next month?"

Two Buttons protested. "Ah, no, Jenny. We've had too many 'next weeks'!"

"Then," said Jenny resolutely, "tomorrow! I'll burn the candle and sew all night!"

"But your dress was finished, Jenny, months ago!"

Jenny looked at him in amazement. "Do you think a girl can marry a duke in a plain dress? I must sew on braids and pearls!"

Two Buttons took her hand in his and said, "I've beaded many a boot and buskin, so I'll help you."

When they returned to the assembled people and announced that tomorrow would be their wedding day, there was a great shout of joy. The King said he would stay in Trisket to attend the festivities, and Howard the Miller, overcome with importance and generosity, insisted that His Majesty must be his honored guest, since his was the largest house in Trisket and conveniently adjacent to the church.

Two Buttons, as the new Duke of Coldwater, hired the warden and his guardsmen on the spot and assigned them to guard the royal person as Edward and his wife Margaret led their majestic guest to his billet.

And so Jenny and her Duke were married the next day with the King himself reading the lessons on request of the parish priest.

Through the years that followed the Duke of Coldwater went about helping the King's people and, on occasion, mending a pair of shoes if it was needed. Generous and fair he was called, loyal and dependable. But forever he was remembered as the Purple Duke who had once been the cobbler, Two Buttons.

The Princess with Wooden Ears

A Little Germanic Kingdom, 1750

Many years ago in the Kingdom of Westerlitz, the people anxiously awaited news from the royal palace, for it was whispered that the young Emperor and Empress were expecting their first child. Emperor Heinrich Johann had already approved preparations to celebrate this great event.

One can imagine the feelings of the poor Emperor, who had hoped it would be a little prince, when he heard from the royal doctor that not only was his child a girl, but also that she was an unfortunate little baby who was born without ears.

"What! Not any?" cried the Emperor. "Not even tiny ones? Little ones that, in time, might grow?"

"None at all, Your Majesty," Dr. Braunschlauf replied regretfully. "The little Princess is doomed to go through life without any ears. But—be of good cheer. Your baby is in every other way healthy. Her mother is beautiful and her father handsome; she cannot possibly be ugly."

"True," conceded Emperor Heinrich Johann. Then he jumped from his throne as if stung by a bee. "Where, oh where," he demanded, "will we find a prince who will marry a princess without any ears?"

The doctor looked puzzled and the Prime Minister nonplussed. The Empress, however, was not at all worried about the future of the little princess. "Come, smile," she coaxed her husband. "Aren't you happy to have a little princess to liven up the gloomy palaces?"

"Oh, yes, Katrina!" the Emperor agreed, hastily. But still in the back of his mind was the question: Can a princess be happy without any ears?

As the days passed, the Empress guessed what worried her husband. Finally she said, "Come, Heinrich. We must plan to make life rollicking and gay for our little earless one."

"But how, Katrina, how?" asked Heinrich Johann.

The Empress pulled the pins from her crown of plaited golden hair. "First," she said, "you must make it unlawful for little girls to wear braids, and for women to appear in public showing their ears. I shall train our little darling's hair into curls on either side of her face. Then it will be fashionable for little girls to wear Princess Fredericka curls."

And so began the campaign to keep Princess Fredericka from learning about ears. The Empress herself set the style for women by combing her hair into little puffs over each ear. No pain or discomfort was spared to keep the little princess from discovering that other people had ears.

The Emperor, meanwhile, called in his Prime Minister, Count Schlizkopf, to help prepare the royal decree concerning ears. But, after working diligently on it for a day and a half, Count Schlizkopf appeared before his Emperor, worn down with worry. "The decree, Your Imperial Majesty," he blurted out, "contains the word 'ears' no less than four times. He who reads the decree will himself be breaking the law."

"Where? How?" blustered Heinrich Johann. "That is impossible."

The round little Prime Minister adjusted his glasses. "Not at all, your Highness, I assure you. Just listen: 'Anyone speaking aloud the word "EARS" within the borders of the Westerlitzian Empire shall pay for his folly by losing his head.' I ask you as an old friend, Heinrich, who wants to read such a decree?"

The Emperor rubbed his chin thoughtfully for a moment, then smiled brightly. "Don't let that worry you, Schlizkopf old man," he said reassuringly. "I'll give you two weeks' leave to travel throughout Westerlitz, carrying the royal proclamation. As an agent of the Emperor, you will be immune from the law."

So Count Schlizkopf travelled far and wide throughout the land, announcing, "Hear a mandate from his Imperial Highness, Emperor Heinrich Johann: Because his daughter, the Princess Fredericka, has been born without aural appendages, the word "EARS" has been erased from the written and spoken vocabulary of all Westerlitzians. Anyone speaking aloud the word "EARS" within the boundaries of the Westerlitzian Empire shall pay for his folly by losing his head!"

In every public square the populace assembled to hear the decree; they listened intently, then nodded their heads in approval. They all agreed that Princess Fredericka must have no unhappiness visited upon her because she lacked ears. Soon, all Westerlitz was in sympathy with the little princess who had no—well, who hadn't any of "those things"—aural appendages.

All went well, and the little princess grew to be the happiest child in the land. Even the toymakers had taken Princess Fredericka's plight to heart, and they carved heads for little girls' dolls with lovely wooden curls, and never a trace of you-know-what.

"That word" was crossed from schoolmasters' spelling lists, and all writers and printers began dutifully omitting it from their stories, because it soon came time for Fredericka to learn to read and write. Everyone in the land conspired to prevent the embarrasing discovery of "those things" by the little princess—though some mothers became impatient, trying to persuade their little boys to wash "them", without calling them by name.

The Emperor and Empress sometimes found it a little ridiculous, talking in circles to avoid mentioning aural appendages. The strain was greatest for them because, as the Empress often said, they had to set an example for the populace. And because the princess was part of their family, they lived in constant dread that it would be they who broke the law.

Even the best-guarded secrets have a way of popping out most unexpectedly, with no one at fault. And, fortunately for everyone's heads, it was the Emperor himself who had to break the silence about ears.

It happened that an old minstrel, travelling from castle to castle to entertain the royal courts with his songs and stories, came to the Emperor's palace on one of his annual visits. Of course Frostbenner, the minstrel, knew about the ban on the mention of ears and had changed his ditties accordingly. But he was an old man, and he forgot that some words might arouse the curiosity of a little child. When the Westerlitzian court had assembled in the throne room, the Emperor and Empress entered and sat down, with Princess Fredericka between them.

Frostbenner struck a few notes, tuning his mandolin, and then began his ballad:

Hear the tale of the water lily,
Hear how the maiden pined away
Hear how the wicked old witch, Dame Henda,
Doomed Alyse in the water to stay.

Now the little princess knew what it was to hear because, thank Fortune, although she had no ears, she could hear very well. But no one had ever mentioned hearing before in her presence, and now a sudden thought struck her. She turned to her father, the Emperor, and asked, "Father, how do we hear?"

The innocent question came as a thunderclap to the Emperor. His heart froze. His face grew red. What could he do? What could he say? He opened his mouth but he could not speak.

The Empress, quick-witted and clever, saw what difficulty troubled her husband. Immediately she called out, "His Majesty, the Emperor, has been taken ill! Doctor Braunschlauf, help the Emperor to his apartments! Clear the throne room! Summon the guards!"

In the midst of the confusion that billowed up around her, little Fredericka stood frozen with terror. Chairs tilted and toppled; skirts, lifted too late, were trampled and torn. Just as she was about to be swept up in the stampede, her nurse, Anneka, reached her side and pulled her to safety. Across the boiling throne room Anneka called to the Empress, "I am here. Your Highness! I will take care of my Princess!"

"Good, Anneka!" replied the Empress. "I must hurry to my husband. He needs me!"

Once behind closed doors, Emperor Heinrich Johann thrashed about in agony. "What shall I tell my daughter? Count Schlizkopf, you are the wisest man in all Westerlitz. How can I explain about hearing to Fredericka, without mentioning our means of hearing?"

The little old man seemed to crumble under the weight of the burden now thrust upon him. "Please, Heinrich," be begged, "I must have quiet so I can think." The Emperor raised a cautioning hand, crossed his lips with a forefinger, and darted an admonishing glance to everyone around him. Count Schlizkopf frowned over the rims of his spectacles. "HMMMMmmmmm, aaaaaAAAAA!" he murmured to himself. "No, that way is out—It's just too—too—impossible." Abruptly, a grin stole up his wrinkled face, from pointed chin to shiny forehead. "I've got it!" he said, bouncing up and down. "An idea at last, Heinrich! You can tell the Princess that we hear with the ear drum. That's it, Heinrich, the ear drum!"

Everyone gasped. At that moment, the Count recognized his error and its consequences. He sank into a chair, his head in his hands. "Ach, no! I have said that word! And now off comes the head!"

The Emperor exploded over this display of weakness. "Don't speak such nonsense, Schlizkopf. I won't permit you to be beheaded before you give me an explanation for Princess Fredericka!"

A victim of his own words, the Count blubbered on: "Your Highness! Royal Emperor! Nobody can tell about hearing without mentioning ears. There! I've said it again, and I'm glad! Now maybe this foolishness will cease. There is nothing left to do but tell the Princess what ears are. She has asked you a question and you must be honest with her!"

"Now I really am sick," groaned the Emperor in disgust. "Drag him away!"

Before the guards could lay a hand on the little man, the Empress took command. She turned to her husband and said, "Heinrich, a moment, please. Count Schlizkopf is right. We must be honest with Fredericka. Who knows, she may be proud of having no ears. This she must decide for herself. But she must have an answer to her question, Heinrich. Abolish the decree, and let our Fredericka know what ears are."

The Emperor sat up. He saw the wisdom in his wife's words. Straightway he sent for his daughter. "We hear, dear Fredericka," he announced, "with our ears."

"Our ears?" little Fredericka repeated. "I do not know what ears are, Papa." With a smile on her face, she sat on her father's knee, patiently waiting for the Emperor's explanation.

But the poor Emperor could only stammer, "Ears are—ears are—" he choked and sputtered, unable to explain. Again, the Empress came to his rescue.

"I will show you, Fredericka," she said. "Come close, little one. Now lift the bun of hair on the left side of my head."

The Princess did as she was bid. She gasped in pleasure. "It's the prettiest think I have ever seen! It's like—a sea shell." She reached up and touched her mother's ear. Without ornament or jewel, it was most certainly the prettiest object in sight.

A half-minute passed before Fredericka withdrew her hand. Her fingers fluttered uncertainly as they crept up to explore, under her curls, the side of her head. Her face clouded with disappointment. "I don't have any," she murmured. She turned to the Emperor. "Do you have ears, Papa? Let me lift your wig and see if you—. You do!"

The little girl was discovering the truth. She ran to her friend, Count Schlizkopf. "Take off your cap, Count Schlizkopf! No, don't turn away! I must see; I must know." The poor Prime Minister hung his head as Fredericka's fingers confirmed her suspicions. "You, too!" she wailed. "Everyone has them, excepting me, and I want ears! I want them so!"

On hearing this cry of anguish, the Emperor sank deeper into his pillows, while the Empress wept into her silk handkerchief. Dr. Braunschlauf hurried to their side, ready to give them medical assistance, if need be.

Anneka went to the little princess and swooped her up into strong arms. "Hush, little one," the nurse crooned. "You shall have ears, if I have to make them myself." Fredericka looked up, her weeping stilled by Anneka's words.

"Make them?" Fredericka asked.

Emperor Heinrich Johann sat up in bed; he gasped "Make them!" And Count Schlizkopf sputtered "Make them?" while Dr. Braunschlauf stamped his foot on the polished floor and thundered "Make ears? Impossible!"

The Emperor, recovering suddenly from his illness, swung his legs over the side of his bed. "Not at all impossible!" he proclaimed with a broad smile. "Ears are made every day, and often right under our very noses. We'll call in the court sculptors and have them make ears out of stone."

Empress Katrina tossed her handkerchief aside, protesting "Too heavy, Heinrich! The ears should be made of wax so that they can be attached easily to Fredericka's head."

"Wax ears would melt and drip like candles," snapped Heinrich Johann.

"But can't you understand how cold and uncomfortable stone ears must be?" chided his wife.

Into this imperial disagreement Anneka presented a suggestion for compromise. "Why not combine the virtue of both plans, Your Highnesses, and have the ears made of wood? Wood is more permanent than wax, yet lighter in weight than stone. And I'm sure our craftsmen will find a comfortable way to attach Princess Fredericka's ears."

The Empress beamed with approval and the Emperor nodded in agreement. "I know just the person to make them," he declared. "Remember the dollmaker, old Herr Shiller? He has carved many a beautiful ear. He will give you ears, Fredericka."

The little Princess stood there in the circle of smiles. "Well," she began uncertainly, "if they are as pretty as Mama's, I'll be satisfied with wooden ears."

"Beautiful!" sang the Empress, whirling her daughter round in a little waltz. "We'll send for Shiller today, and I will model for him as he carves."

The Emperor stood up, put on his shoes and buttoned the collar of his uniform. "Everything has turned out so well that now I am well," he declared. He turned to his Prime Minister. "Schlizkopf, release the minstrel. Frostbenner has really done us a great favor. I don't think I could have stood the strain of "ears" another day!"

And that was the way matters stood. Everyone seemed quite pleased with the turn of events. Frostbenner was rewarded instead of being executed, and the Emperor took to talking of the matter quite lightly.

"Well, you see," he would explain to one or another of the members of the Court, "there were so many solutions to the problem. Naturally, I can't ask my people to chop off their ears because my little daughter happens to have none." So the ban against mention of ears faded away, but Princess Fredericka curls were thought so attractive that the style stayed in vogue for many a year.

Meanwhile, the Empress sat happily modeling her ears. In no time at all, she was telling the dollmaker, "They are excellent likenesses, Shiller. Just soften this curve here, and they will be perfect."

With everybody so busy trying to make her happy, Princess Fredericka finally gave in and smiled, and she was once more the carefree little girl she was before she discovered what ears were.

At last the day came when Shiller finished his work on the exquisite wooden ears. The Empress hurried with them to the royal library where Fredericka was reading a story for Anneka.

"Here they are, dear one," sang mother to daughter. "Let us see how well they fit." The Empress slipped the thin gold wire holding the ears together over the top of Fredericka's head and between her curls; with a little snap each ear popped into place. The little princess's wish had been granted.

Anneka patted Fredericka's curls. "Perfect, Your Highness," she said. "The blessed!"

"Exquisite!" murmured the Empress in agreement. "At last my little darling has ears!"

Fredericka sighed as she picked up her book and prepared to go on with her reading. From that moment on, she was determined to be a happy little princess with wooden ears.

The Empress reported to the Emperor that their daughter was at last content with her new ears, and the Emperor sensed that a new feeling of well-being had come to the imperial household. Never before had he known everyone to be happy at one and the same time, and he was moved to issue a proclamation naming the coming decade the Era of Frederickian Contentment.

As she grew up, Fredericka became lovelier with each passing year. Now that she had grown used to her wooden ears, she did not mind their peeping from behind her bouncing curls while she rode her favorite horse at a fast pace over the royal domain. She was followed on these wild chases by her faithful nurse and companion, Anneka who, truth to tell, was almost as expert a horsewoman as was the Princess.

But how loudly Anneka protested against the bone-jolting speed! "Princess Fredericka!" she shouted. "Do slow down! How can you expect a woman of my age to go flying over the countryside? In future, I shall insist on your riding with one of the grooms instead of your old nurse."

"No, no, no!" shrieked Fredericka. "I won't hear your lecture about being an old woman!" But she did reign in the horse, bringing him to a dancing trot. "I've heard that complaint too often, and I know you just want me to protest how young you look."

Anneka, taking advantage of the slower gait to pull her jacket straighter over her shoulders, said, "A woman has a little vanity, even if she daren't have any pride. Look how my hair has fallen."

Fredericka watched as Anneka tried to repair the damage. "Two twists and a few pins and it will be as neat as ever," she assured Anneka. She turned in her saddle to survey the fields through which they had just ridden. "What a wonderful day for frisking over the countryside!"

Anneka agreed. "Beautiful!" she said. "But I know half of your pleasure is in avoiding having to listen to Prince Ivan again."

"You have to listen to Ivan as long as I have to. And you don't enjoy his bragging any more than I." Fredericka pulled down her jaw and lowered his voice in imitation of the Russian Prince. "My dear Prancess, in Rawsha ve do not hawv sooch hawt vethair!"

Anneka clucked her tongue. "You are unkind to the poor Prince. He may yet be the best choice among your suitors. *Every* prince cannot be dashing and handsome."

Princess Fredericka's pretty face wore a troubled frown. "What you say is true, Anneka. But the man I marry must think of someone besides himself. He should be generous and good."

"And a prince, don't forget."

Fredericka pouted.

"I'm afraid you won't find all those qualities and requirements in one human being. You may find yourself betrothed to a prince who is good but not generous; or generous enough, but thoughtless and insensitive."

Fredericka gave an angry little cry. "We won't talk of it any more, Anneka! I want to enjoy my afternoon." She whirled her horse about in a little circle. Then, abandoning the unpleasant topic and throwing off the fretful mood, Fredericka sang out happily. "Just think! Next week I'll be eighteen, and oh! What a wonderful birthday ball Mother has planned. At last I'm to dance with the Emperor, Anneka! Poor Papa! He has grown a little stout, and he is afraid he will get out of breath."

"You have danced with your father a hundred times!"

"Oh, but it's not the same," Fredericka protested. "This time I shall be a grown-up lady, dancing with His Majesty before the whole court."

Anneka had been looking at the shadows cast by trees in the hedgerow along the side of the field. "Well," she said, "it's time for the grown-up young lady to go home for a rest. His Majesty will hold a long audience this evening, and you must attend. It has been rumored that Prince Oskar of Norway and Prince Jan of the Netherlands will arrive in time to be presented. And I want you to look your best."

Fredericka began to protest, but Anneka was firm. "We'll have no excuses! Home for a nap! If you don't need one, I do. I'm worn out trying to keep up with you."

The Princess rode back to the palace where Anneka prepared her for the royal nap. With drapes drawn over the windows, Fredericka lay a while on cool satin pillows, not ready to sleep; there were so many things to think about!

"I don't know whether I like this growing up." But having admitted her indecision, Fredericka began to look for the brighter side of her situation. "I must do what is right for a Westerlitzian princess. Papa says I will be Empress one day and he will help me find a consort who will make me happy and serve the Empire well. Perhaps Prince Oskar will be more pleasant than Ivan has been. I hope so! I don't want to choose Ivan. And I am told that the Dutch Prince, Jan is a delightful person. But we shall see, we shall see. Of course, I must look my prettiest for my Birthday Ball. I think I shall have a little surprise for the fine Princes."

The Princess smiled as she patted her curls and pillowed her cheek with her hand. "I shall wear my hair swept up to the top of my head, and show my pretty carved ears. No other girl in the whole of Westerlitz will be wearing her hair like that." Fredericka, pleased with her plans, sighed in contentment. "It will make me look so different. And I do want to have everyone notice me at my Birthday Ball." She drifted into sleep.

Fredericka lay there napping for two hours, perhaps longer. Abruptly, Anneka came storming in from the ante-chamber. "Fredericka! Princess, wake up! You have slept long past your usual time. It's my fault! I dropped off myself after I laid out your clothes for the evening. Your father has sent a page for you, and he will be angry when he learns I have allowed you to oversleep!"

Fredericka, now fully awake, began to dress swiftly but carefully. As she pulled on petticoats and underblouses, she tried to comfort her companion. "Papa has never been impatient with me—or with you, for that matter."

Anneka, accustomed for years to helping the Princess dress, handed her each piece of clothing and deftly helped with buttons and hooks. Still she bemoaned her lapse in duty.

"Hush, Anneka!" said the Princess. "No one has lost his head in Westerlitz during my lifetime. Here, tie this bow and my overskirt will hang just right. You go on like an old woman, Anneka! Now, let me have my stockings!"

Anneka produced the stockings as commanded. "The page says that all three Princes will dine with you. Norway and Holland arrived a half hour ago, and Russia is bellowing that he is hungry."

"My shoes, Anneka!" Fredericka stepped into them and there she was—a beautifully dressed princess. She gave her old nurse a hug. "Quickly, now," she said, "send the page back to Papa and I'll hurry down the back stairs."

In the marble-columned foyer below, Emperor Heinrich Johann stood waiting with his newly-arrived royal guests, for his wife and daughter. "I am happy to welcome you, Jan and Oskar. Prince Ivan of Russia has been here for several days and has already met my daughter Fredericka. He who wins my daughter will rule at her side one day. Now you must tell me, have you had a pleasant journey?"

The bearded and moustached Norwegian Prince Oskar, looking fierce as a Viking from old Norse legends, spoke up, assuring the Emperor that he had enjoyed every mile of the way. "I met Jan in Amsterdam, Your Majesty, and together we have crossed Germany and on into your beautiful country."

Jan of the Netherlands, slighter and darker but just as tall as Oskar, added his impression of Westerlitz. "Your clean little villages remind me of home, although you have no windmills or dikes. Westerlitz is very pretty."

Oskar, not to be outdone, pulled the monocle from his left eye and waved it in a graceful arc. "But Katriniensbourg!" he gasped. "It is the Queen of Cities! And your palace is the finest gem she wears!" he restored the monocle to his eye. "Such splendor! It takes one's breath away!"

The Emperor beamed; here was conversation to his liking. "I am pleased, gentle Princes, that you have found so much of interest in our wonderful Westerlitz. Only when our capital city became as beautiful as my Empress, Katrina, would I permit it to be named for her."

Here, thought Prince Jan, is a great Emperor, by turns modest and boastful, willing to concede to the wishes of his people, but not one moment before his standards were met.

"And here," thought Prince Oskar, "is my opportunity to insure my future, my name written in history books. I shall be the powerful Prince Consort—the strength behind the throne. If only the Princess has the least bit of beauty and grace!"

Princess Fredericka appeared at the doorway and Oskar's monocle dropped from his eye, so amazing was her beauty and grace. Now she glided to the Emperor's side, singing "Good evening, Papa!" as she kissed his cheek. "I hope I have not kept you waiting!"

"No, no," the Emperor assured her as he gave her a hug. He

turned to the Princes, who stood at attention. "Here are some new friends for you, little one. From the fjords of his native land comes Prince Oskar of Norway."

Oskar, aware of the glittering impression his uniform was making on the girl-Princess, clicked his heels and bowed, tilting his head ever so slightly, and burst into speech: "Delighted to meet you at last, my Princess! I have just been exclaiming over the breathtaking beauty of Katriniensbourg!"

Fredericka, her hand in Oskar's, curtsied low and murmured "How charming, Prince Oskar."

And lest the Dutch Prince feel overshadowed by the dashing and handsome Norwegian, the Emperor of Westerlitz loudly proclaimed "And here is Prince Jan of the Netherlands!"

Plainly dressed and with only his smile to brighten his appearance, Jan took Fredericka's hand in his and turned to Heinrich Johann. "It is your daughter who takes my breath away, Your Majesty." Fredericka tilted her head demurely.

Oskar, just a moment too late, tried to out-maneuver Jan by declaring, "Holland has taken the words from my mouth, Princess."

But the Emperor appeared to take no notice of either statement. "The Empress takes a very long time to dress for dinner, but when she comes down you will see where Fredericka gets her beauty."

A young page hurriedly entered and announced "Her Imperial Majesty, Katrina Marie, and the Russian Prince, Ivan!"

The Empress, wearing a bell of skirts, swept into the foyer, her jewels both reflecting and rivalling the many candles in sconces and chandeliers. The Emperor fumbled with his large gold pocket watch and complained, "Katrina, my dear, you have kept us waiting."

But the Empress only smiled and said, "Good evening, Heinrich. I have kept Prince Ivan waiting, too." She was a plumper Empress now, with a touch of silver in the hair that framed her face, but not a bit less lovely or friendly. "And these are our guests," she asked, "from Norway and the Netherlands?"

"Come along," the Emperor urged, taking great bounding steps toward doors opening onto the Emperial banquet hall. "I shall present them to you at dinner!" The carved panels swung open as he approached them and the royal family and their guests swept into the vast pink and gold dining salon.

As they sat around the great gold table, each of the Princes tried his best to beguile pretty Fredericka, to win her attention with brilliant conversation.

"But, Prince Ivan," Fredericka interrupted the Russian's discourse, "I understand from my reading that the Steppes are a great frozen wasteland."

Ivan tilted up his chin and said, "So it is commonly thought, Your Highness. The Steppes hold a great and savage splendor, full of life and pageantry! The roaming peoples thrive on color and excitement. Of course, one so delicate as you would never travel into the Steppes. But I have seen with my own eyes, Princess, such wild and mystic dances in such colorful bazaars that I thought an artist must have spilled his paint-pots!"

Fredericka was amused by Ivan's pompous recitation, but she smiled graciously and said meekly, "I am sorry I am a frail girl, Prince Ivan. I should so enjoy seeing your Steppes." Then she turned to Prince Oskar and added, "And the fjords of Norway, too."

Oskar of Norway, happy for the opportunity to compete with Russia, launched into his lecture. "The fjords, dear Fredericka, run heavy with the finest fish in the world. I have myself gone fishing for weeks on end. But the open rolling sea is the real fishing ground for a Norwegian fisherman! When the sky is blue and the water bluer still, you would love it, my Princess! "

"I'm sure I would, Oskar," said Fredericka, and she turned to Jan. "What does a Dutch prince do to wile away the hours?"

Jan smiled modestly and told her, "There are few hours to wile away, Fredericka. My Hollanders have taken their land from the bottom of the sea. We, too, love the water, but we must keep it out of our fields and homes with our dikes. Our windmills pump water from the rivers to keep them from flooding. I have worked with the millers, Fredericka, just as Oskar has with his fishermen. In idle moments I have attached a little grinding wheel to the great shaft of the windmill. I have learned to cut and polish diamonds, like this one I have brought you." He pulled a little leather pouch from a pocket attached to his belt and placed it in Fredericka's hand.

Fredericka tipped out the contents of the pouch and the diamond spun into a glittering dance on the table cloth. It was large and round, with the fire of a star. Fredericka was delighted. "Oh, it is beautiful, Jan! How it sparkles in the candlelight!"

Empress Katrina gasped in pleasure. "A finer gem I have never seen!" she declared. "It is worth a fortune, Prince Jan!" The Emperor, too, was impressed and commented on the perfect shape.

But Prince Ivan turned a fishy eye on the splendid diamond, sneering, "We too have gems in Russia, but our princes need not polish them to earn a living."

Jan turned to Ivan. "You misunderstand, Prince Ivan. I have done this work to help establish the craft in Holland, to make life easier for our craftsmen. We are learning to do better all the time." Now he turned to Emperor Heinrich Johann. "See, here is another, Your Highness—a sapphire from Africa!"

The Emperor could only murmur "Magnificent!" as he turned the blue beauty this way and that, to catch the watery flashings from the faceted depths.

Ivan, wild with jealousy, leaped from his chair and stood towering over the table. He shouted, "I hope I may be allowed to present the sable and ermine furs I chose for the Princess!"

Empress Katrina, sensing that an international disagreement could arise and destroy the friendly relations among nations, swept to her feet and with taste, wisdom and charm, brought harmony back to the dinner party. "Of course, Ivan," she said. "No time would be better than right now. You and

Oskar may follow Jan's example and make your presentations. Then Fredericka can wear all your lovely gifts next Saturday evening for her Birthday Ball."

The tension relaxed and the Emperor sighed in relief. The delicate balance of power had been preserved by Katrina Marie's diplomatic suggestion.

The days flew by with their banquets and parties, with the Imperial parents constantly alert to the exigencies of protocol. At last came the day of the Birthday Ball.

Fredericka, remembering her plan to surprise all those who attended the ball, sent Anneka to help the coatroom maids. Thus the Princess was free to dress herself leisurely; now she began to arrange her hair to best display her lovely wooden ears. "None will have such pretty ears as I," she thought. As she slipped pins and combs into her curls to hold them in place, she permitted her vanity to add "And I shall be the first to wear my hair combed high!"

In the distance a choir of trumpets pealed out fanfares. This was Fredericka's signal that all the guests had been assembled and it was now time for her to make her appearance. She stood one last moment before the mirror. "I do hope my train hangs properly!" she breathed, and she swept along the gallery to the top of the stairs.

The state ballroom of Westerlitz was spacious and high, with entrances on the ground level for guests, and a great sweeping staircase descending from the royal apartments and bedrooms.

Now Fredericka descended the marble stairs, slowly and majestically. She felt every inch a princess, the object of everyone's admiration and affection. She knew that she was pretty because she had been told that ever so many times; now she found the great company of court members and royal guests bowing low and curtsying. She felt truly elegant.

One little duchess looked up and saw what she had never seen before, Fredericka's artificial ears. "Her ears! Her ears!" exclaimed the duchess; she tittered, then fainted. Someone else, close by and seeing the beautiful carved appendages, took up the cry "Oh look, oh look at her ears!" Another giggled openly, then hid her face in her handkerchief. Soon everyone was laughing.

"Why," Fredericka thought, "they are laughing at me!" She ran to the Emperor and cried, "Make them stop laughing, Papa! They are laughing at my ears!"

The Emperor waved his arms and, finding that he could not control the crowd, he beckoned for his Prime Minister. "Silence them, Schlizkopf!" was the Imperial command.

"There is only one thing to do," advised the little old Prime Minister. "Start the dancing!" he hurried to the bandmaster and orderd the musicians to play a lively tune.

The Emperor, for the first time annoyed with his daughter, began to scold. "Whatever possessed you, Fredericka! You have made yourself a spectacle!"

Fredericka whimpered. "I didn't know it would be like this. I wanted to surprise everyone."

"That you certainly have!" snapped Katrina Marie, every inch the angry Empress. Her eyes blazed; she could think of nothing more to say.

The Emperor tried to comfort his daughter. "This hurt will pass, little Princess. It will make no difference to those who really care for you. Here, drop your curls and everyone will forget this unfortunate incident."

But Heinrich Johann spoke too soon. Prince Oskar stood at his elbow. "Your Imperial Highness, I must have a word with you."

"But certainly, my boy," said the Emperor.

Prince Oskar screwed the monocle into his eye and began. "As you are aware, Sire, I am second son to the King of Norway. I may, some day, be called to the throne, and Norway may not have a queen without her own ears."

Emperor Heinrich Johann rubbed his chin thoughtfully; he now saw how things were going. "I see. And you are withdrawing your offer of marriage to Princess Fredericka?"

"Unfortunately, I must," said Oskar. "The offer would never have been made if our foreign minister had been told all. But, under the circumstances—."

Here, Prince Ivan of Russia burst into the conversation. "Your Excellency!" he screamed. Oskar, insulted by Ivan's rude interruption, dropped his monocle, and indignantly withdrew. Heinrich Johann turned to Ivan. "Your Excellency," yelped Ivan, "I protest your deceit in concealing Princess Fredericka's deformity!"

The Emperor tried to shield his daughter by urging the Prince to discuss the matter quietly. But, failing in this effort, he asked, "And you, too, wish to withdraw your proposal of marriage?"

Wily and scheming, Ivan replied, "I have not said that in so many words, Your Highness. But I feel I must have a greater reward if I accept a princess without ears as my wife."

The Emperor was puzzled. "So?" he asked. "And what would you require?"

Ivan, with angry eyes flashing, demanded "You must rename the capital of Westerlitz for *me*. Ivansbourg would be very appropriate if I am to be Fredericka's Consort. And I must have complete control of the Treasury."

Stung by Ivan's impertinence, Emperor Heinrich Johann ordered him to leave Westerlitz at once.

"Very well, Your Excellency," hissed Ivan, "I shall leave you to your daughter with wooden ears!"

The Emperor looked about him. He had never seen such a situation in all his years. Empress Katrina and Princess Fredericka, having forgiven each other, were weeping openly. Two angry Princes were plowing their way through the whirling dancers on the ballroom floor; his Prime Minister was hurrying along at their coattails, trying to restore international tranquility.

"Oh, Papa!" wailed Fredericka as she turned to him. "I heard them! I couldn't help hearing them with my wooden ears!" She buried her head in her father's shoulder and was about to weep afresh when she felt someone touch her arm. Looking up, she saw that Prince Jan was standing at her elbow.

"Dry your tears, Fredericka," Jan said. "Come dance with me."

Fredericka put her hand on his arm and Jan led her to the dance floor. She smiled at him as they took their first step. "Jan," she asked, "aren't you ashamed to be seen with a princess whose ears are of carved wood?"

"My mother always taught me that those who show their shortcomings are more honest than those who hide them."

Fredericka considered this philosophy before she asked, "And you would marry me?"

The Dutch Prince said, "I will marry you if I am honored with your love, Fredericka. I am only second cousin to the ruler of the Netherlands, but I will try to be a good husband for you." The Princess with wooden ears hesitated to reply and Jan added, "You need not worry about being the Princess with Wooden Ears any longer. I have in my pocket two big Dutch gold coins. I have learned the goldsmith's trade and I shall beat the coins into golden ears for my princess."

Fredericka danced away her sadness. And, next morning, she went hand-in-hand with Prince Jan to the Imperial goldsmith's shop where he worked happily an hour, beating the gold into shape.

"Listen, Jan," sang Fredericka, "to the ring of the gold on the anvil."

Prince Jan gave two final taps and said, "There! They are finished. May they always bring music to you, dear Fredericka."

Fredericka and Jan were married with great pomp and splendor, and the sad little tale of the Princess with Wooden Ears was forgotten until this very day.